SORCER
BOOK TWO OF THE
S

Robert Ryan

Cover design by www.damonza.com

ISBN: 9798284011010
(print edition)

Trotting Fox Press

Contents

1. The First Sign

The storm, now fading, still muttered in the distance. Yet the powerful rumble of it was less ominous than the words spoken by Cadawn.

All around, the skies darkened as dusk rushed on. The tattered remnants of the cloud-wrack drew across the sky like the ragged banners of a defeated army, and the last light of the westering sun dyed them as blood, and then the world fell into darkness.

Drom looked at the face of the druid, pale and pained in the shadows, and he knew that questions must wait. But he would hear more of the prophecy. How could a priestess and a warrior return a god to life? Worse. It was not a prophecy that they would, but only that they would attempt to. And if they failed, darkness and evil would follow forever.

Lightning flashed in the distance, and the remains of the knife the gortha had flung became visible against the ground. The last of it dissolved into a gray vapor, and there was a scent of bitterness.

"There was poison on that blade," Ariane said.

Cadawn straightened. He seemed weak, but determination stiffened him like wind in a sail. At some point he had stuffed cloth under his tunic and over the wound to staunch any bleeding. Drom did not think that was the danger though.

"There was sorcery too," the druid said. "I must get back to my people. They'll help. There are those among them who know the enchantments of faery better than I, and how to counter them."

A moment the druid took to collect the two pieces of the broken staff, and almost reverently he picked up the two iron bands that had fallen off the ends. Then Drom helped the druid mount his horse, and he noticed that the arm that had been injured seemed limp and cold to touch.

They rode slowly then despite their urgency. Cadawn would not likely stay mounted if they went faster, and the ground was slicked by rain and dangerous.

It was fortunate that the druid's horse seemed to know the way well. Cadawn did not guide it, but by instinct and long experience in the swamp it found a sure path.

In the distance the storm muttered angrily, but ever it faded and the stars kindled above. By their light, and the far-away flashes of lightning, Drom and Ariane sometimes exchanged glances. They both worried about the druid.

Cadawn began to slump in the saddle, and Drom determined to keep him awake if the cause were just tiredness. If it were poison, it would need skill greater than his own or any talent Ariane had.

"You talked about prophecy, Cadawn. What is it, and what has it to do with your broken staff?"

The druid sat a little straighter in the saddle.

"It has everything to do with the staff. Its breaking is the first great sign that the days of testing have begun. The prophecy was made near the founding of the kingdom by one of the great druids. Conhain he was called, and the staff was the very one that he bore, and the archdruids before him back into the dark days before even the Shadowed Wars."

The druid reached back to touch his saddle bags where the broken staff was stowed.

"It has passed through many hands until mine, and it was Conhain who won the two metal bands, the *hathlinden* as they are called, from the hoard of the dragon Rah-essen. A great feat in its own right, and he was aided by the hero

4

Rathglen also. Rathglen perished, but Conhain lived on, and accomplished other feats. Some even greater."

The far horizon lit up with a streak of lightning, but the remnants of the storm had drifted so far away now that no thunder could be heard.

"From Conhain comes the prophecy. When the staff breaks, it will be the end of a druidic age. Destiny will be in a state of flux, and Aroth will live again. Or the world will sink into darkness."

Cadawn swayed in the saddle, then regained his composure. They did not question him more, but Drom rode close and was ready to assist him if he fell.

The druid was stronger than he looked though. Through the night they rode, and he sat like a stone in the saddle. Ungraceful as a rider maybe, yet he did not topple.

It was clear though that he was gravely ill as the first gray light of the next morning slowly lit the world. His face was deathly pale, his eyes sunken, and he shivered as one in a fever.

"Can you do nothing for him?" Drom whispered to Ariane as their mounts neared when the path widened.

She shook her head. "I can help heal ordinary hurts. And I have some power against evil, or those under the shadow of it. Against faery magic though, which often is neither of the Light nor the Dark, I have no power. Still less when I don't understand the nature of the hurt."

Drom was worried. He had seen men sicken and die before, and Cadawn had an unwholesome look about him. It was by strength of will alone that he remained in the saddle, and not strength of body. In his experience though, when the latter failed the first followed not long after.

Even as Drom thought of stopping to make a fire and warm the druid, and perhaps give him a little strength by getting him to eat, if he could, a strange sound drifted over the swamplands.

It was chanting. Through the morning mists that rose up from the swamp waters all around, a line of men could be seen treading a path over the few dry tracks that they must have known so well.

Drom guessed who they were. Druids. He had seen their kind before in Camalduin, and elsewhere, but those were Court Druids. These men, and he saw some women among them too, were druids of an older order. They traced back even before the Shadowed Wars, and there was a mystique about them. They trod the earth slowly, and their chanting was drawn out and sonorous, yet they were warriors too, in their way. They had powers he could barely guess at. And courage.

He knew the stories. Cadawn had mentioned Conhain earlier, one of the greats of their order, and one which every child in the realm had heard stories about. For the more the Court Druids and the king tried to suppress such things, the more they prospered. If in secret.

Cadawn drew his mount to a halt and waited. In the new light of the sun he looked deathly ill, yet still there was a spark about him as his people came to help. How they knew, Drom could not fathom. Or maybe it was prearranged they should come. Either way, Cadawn sat proudly in his saddle until the druids reached him. They helped him dismount, and those coming behind brought a stretcher and helped him onto it.

An old man approached Drom and Ariane. He pulled back his hood and eyed them carefully. His skin was ancient, and his long hair white as frost. His pale eyes looked like they had seen a hundred summers, yet there was still strength in his wire-thin body.

He bowed. "Greetings, daughter of Aroth. Welcome, O Protector. Your coming has been long awaited."

There was something about the old man that Drom had not seen before but heard of. He seemed almost holy, and there was a peace about him that neither merriment nor disaster could disturb.

"Cadawn has been struck by the blade of a gortha," Ariane said.

The old man bowed again. "This we know, and we will do what we can. We are not without power, even against the magic of faery. Yet the gortha-spell is strong, as the ancient lore tells us."

Drom and Ariane followed the column of druids as they wound their way back, and deeper, into the swamp. The ancient man named himself as Tathgar, but said little more. He stayed near them though, ensuring they did not stray from the narrow path. At times this was exceedingly dangerous, for the path could be so thin that only one horse at a time could traverse it, and at others, where it seemed wider, the apparently solid ground was treacherous bog, only discovered by standing on it.

Several times the old man guided them carefully, and proved the danger by dropping a stone where they would have ridden, and laughing with glee as they watched it sink slowly without trace.

By mid-morning the sun was bright and warm. The mosquitoes still lingered, but were not as bad. The smell remained as it always did, which was unpleasant but unnoticed unless some particularly strong waft of odor was born toward the column on a malignant breeze.

They came to a village. It was established on a higher stretch of land, but only by some twenty feet or so. It was like villages Drom had seen elsewhere in Camlanta in the remotest areas. There were huts, built of strong timber and thatched by thick grasses, or reeds in this case, cleverly laid atop each other to dispel rainfall. Smoke rose from some of the huts, finding a way through a hole at the peak.

Around the village was a circular wall of tall stakes, pointed at the ends, and a heavy-timbered gate on the path facing the column of druids.

The gate opened by unseen hands and the druids filed through. The inhabitants came out of their huts and looked gravely at the stretcher on which Cadawn was carried. Their love for him was obvious, as was their concern. Many did not appear to be druids. There were men and women, farmers, potters, smiths and the usual trades of any villages. The druids dispersed among them, and Cadawn was carried by a few to a central building.

"A place for your rest has been made ready," Tathgar said. He led them to an adjacent hut. "Someone will come at your call if you need anything. In the meanwhile, pray for the deliverance of our brother. He is strong, but he is only human. The gortha was of faery, and ancient in evil."

They thanked him and entered the hut. It was neat inside, with a central firepit, a large table, and two pallets with animal-hide blankets for sleeping. Food was prepared and left on the table.

"They knew we were coming, and that there would be two of us," Drom said.

"Or Cadawn knew and told them before he rode to our aid."

Drom scratched his head. "If he knew what was going to happen, why didn't he bring more help to fight the gortha?"

Ariane lit a candle and placed it in the center of the table.

"Foreknowledge is often incomplete. He may not have known how dangerous it was going to be. Or it was one of his tests as a druid. Either way, he needs our help now."

She sat down and held out her hand. Drom knew she was about to pray, and it was not something he believed in. He did not wish to offend her though.

He sat and took her hand. He never prayed. He gained what he could by his own wit and the skill of his two hands. Why ask the universe for more?

Ariane spoke briefly, voicing her wishes for the recovery of Cadawn. Drom said nothing. Then they remained several moments in silence.

"What will be will be," Ariane said. "But certainly we need Cadawn, and I like him."

Drom did too. The man had great courage. It seemed that Ariane drew such people to her, for the man who had died protecting her back near Drom's old farm was of that sort too.

Courage was all well and good. They would need luck too. It was only at that moment that he realized he would undertake the quest being asked of him. Now that he knew Ariane might be his daughter, he could not refuse.

They ate and then rested. The day drew on, and at whiles they heard chanting from the nearby hut.

"They invoke magic," Ariane said.

Drom was not so sure. The druids had a flavor to them of a religious order. That sort seemed to sing just to pass the hours of the day, but she was not likely to be wrong about her guess either. What powers she had, he did not know. They seemed to be unpredictable, and his knowledge of druids, at least Court Druids, only helped him understand her a little. By the time this was over, if he lived, he would know more.

It was a long night. A wind blew up, and it rushed around the hut with strange hissing sounds. Nearby, the chanting droned on, sometimes falling to near silence and at others growing loud.

Drom slept fitfully, and woke to a quiet dawn. The chanting had ceased and the wind had died. He had a bad feeling that it meant ill news.

Tathgar called to them soon after, and they came out of the dark hut. The sun shone brightly, and the ancient man shook his head.

"It was close," he said. "Closer than it should have been. But in Cadawn we have a druid such as Conhain was. There is strength of iron in him. He will live, and the poison and sorcery of the gortha are dispelled."

Drom felt a thrill run through him. Somehow, he knew this was as it should be. The world needed druids such as that. The vizier would have an opponent.

Ariane grinned broadly. "Can we see him?"

"Tonight," the old man replied. "There'll be a celebration, and a large one. He'll be well enough to talk by then. For now, he sleeps."

It was a long day. Nothing much seemed to happen in the village. Some hunters returned with game, and there was much collecting of timber. Apart from that, it was quiet. The peace reminded Drom of his farm even if the countryside did not.

"Why do they gather so much timber," he asked Ariane.

"The druids like bonfires. Of old, all our people did. The start of summer and of winter was celebrated with great fires and feasts. Now all that many do is to light a candle. Such is the sway of Arofel and the Court Druids. They try to bury the old ways and invent new."

By dusk the village had changed. Anticipation built, and as the sun fell many cheered and sang. Drom and Ariane left their hut, and followed the people as they moved slightly uphill to an area of firm ground close to the village.

It was like a small hill, yet only a little higher than the village. Trees surrounded it, but the center was a clear sward of grass. In the very middle was a ring of standing stones.

In a circle beyond the stones a series of bonfires sprang alight with a cackle of kindling and then a roar as larger branches caught. At first the air was smoky, but it quickly cleared. Then the area for a good way around the stones was lit with a light as though the sun still shone. The stars and night sky were pushed back, and song and laughter burst forth.

A woman came to Drom and Ariane, carrying large clay cups.

"Drink!" she said. "Be merry, for the archdruid remains among us!"

Even as she spoke they saw a new group join them, and Cadawn was among them. He grinned at them and waved, but his face was still pale.

All around them people danced for joy, and when the bonfires burned lower more fuel was added, this time the trunks of the stunted trees that grew freely in the swamps. The light was less, but they burned with great heat.

Drom drank, and he liked it. The cups contained mead, which he preferred even over beer. It was a strong brew though, and on his second cup he began to feel the effects. Ariane narrowed her eyes, but he drank on.

The druids, dour as they seemed, religious as they were, knew how to celebrate. Great cauldrons were brought forth over the coals of one fire, and in them quantities of pork and beef were simmered. For now, they drank and danced. Later they would feast.

Cadawn spoke to them briefly, but he was much in demand and seemed to have many friends, even though this was not his home village in Car Sagoth. To the druids though, that did not matter. He led them all, and all the swamp was their home.

Deep into the evening they ate, but the merriment dwindled little. The mead kept flowing, and when the fires burned low the stars brightened in the night sky like a million distant bonfires.

Drom drank more than he intended. The sweet mead filled his veins, and his mood was merry. Yet he had discovered that he tolerated alcohol better than many. It made him happy rather than aggressive. He could still think cooly, with precise logic, even if his body lost its edge. In the arena this had been important. Sometimes the gladiators drank before a fight to settle their nerves.

Ariane frowned at him from time to time, but he only replied with a wink.

As the gray of dawn filled the skies the druids and the villagers gave a mighty cry, and then slowly wended their way back to their huts. Drom and Ariane went with them, and the first rays of the sun were showing when they passed through the palisade gate.

Cadawn was not to be seen. They had not done so since midnight, and Drom guessed he had spent the second half of the night back in his hut and sleeping. He deserved it, for death had been close.

In his quiet way Tathgar wished them well, and then paused and spoke when they were about to enter their hut.

"Do not think we have forgotten the perils of the outside world," he said. "We have celebrated, for that is our nature. Life is a matter of joy, and the conquest of evil also. Cadawn means much to us, and he took on a task he should not have by himself." He glanced at Ariane then. "You know of what I speak. The spell of raising the dead requires much skill and power. He did it by himself, where normally a half dozen druids would be needed. And he raised a long dead army."

"I know," Ariane said. "The priestesses of Aroth would never attempt it by themselves. None that I have ever heard stories of anyway. We owe him our lives."

The ancient man gazed solemnly at her. "That is so, and yet you will go into greater danger with him yet. Tonight, there will be a meeting in his hut, which you both must go to. And after that, the peril of the world outside the safety of the swamp will be your fate. May Aroth save you, for the powers of the Dark gather against you."

2. The Hathlinden

It was dark in Cadawn's hut. Night had long since fallen over the village, and the only light inside came from the central fire, now burned low to deep embers and the occasional tongues of blue flame.

Drom felt drowsy, but he listened with attention to all that was said. Ariane spoke little, and most of the talking was done by Cadawn and the two druids with him, highest in seniority in the village. Tathgar was one of these.

The scent of herbs was in the air too, and Drom wondered if the druids used something that gave off a drug-smoke. The Court Druids did so, but here the scent was different. He glanced upward. The small aperture at the top of the roof did a good job of channeling away the fumes, and there was little in the room. Perhaps just as well. Or maybe he was just tired from the festivities the previous night.

"You should have let us help you more against the gortha," Ariane was saying.

Cadawn looked down at the fire. "You already did. Yet you are right. Pride got in my way. It will be my task to offer protection against magic, but this quest is one where we all must help each other. That is, assuming we are all agreed to go?" He looked up at those words, and his gaze fell on Drom first.

Drom answered nonchalantly. "I'll go. I had forgotten that adventure could be so … entertaining."

The druid looked at him a few moments longer. Drom had no intention of stating his real reason, mainly that he feared for Ariane. She might be his daughter. Perhaps he would one day discover the truth, and if not he would at least make some atonement for his failings earlier in life. Yet the look Cadawn gave him seemed one of doubt. Was it possible the druid knew more than he told?

Cadawn turned next to Ariane. "And you?"

"Of course. It was for this that I was born. Or rather, every High Priestess of Aroth was born and brought up knowing they might be called upon for this quest. It seems it falls to me though, and I'll not refuse it."

"No matter what it brings?"

"Regardless."

"I shall undertake it as well," the druid said. "All that remains is to decide who else should go, if any."

They discussed that point for a while. It was clear though that they must venture out of Car Sagoth, and that the more they took with them the stronger they would be. Even so, stealth was their best safety. The larger the group the more easily it would be detected, and they all knew that the vizier would continue searching for them relentlessly.

"What will our first task be?" Drom asked. "It seems to me that waking a dead god will be no simple matter."

The village was silent around their hut. Most had gone to sleep now, and all that could be heard from outside was the intermittent call of water hens, loud and piercing in the swamplands.

"Nothing that we do will be simple, and the prophecies are vague. This I know though, for it was the first sign. The Druid Staff is broken, and a new one needed. This Conhain revealed in ages past, and that must be our first quest. My task is to guide and protect, and for that I need the staff foretold for me. It has greater power than the old, and I will need that and more. When we have it, our next step will be clearer."

15

Even as he spoke he glanced at the two metal bands that he had retrieved when his staff was broken, and his look was puzzled.

"Every boy in Camlanta has heard of Conhain," Drom said. "The tales are likely garbled and suppressed though. Tell us more of him? And what he prophesied of us?"

The embers in the fire still burned hot, but it was dark now in the hut and even the cold blue flames had subsided. A few moments Cadawn sat in thought, and then he spoke softly.

"Conhain was one of the greats of our order. Perhaps the greatest ever. Every druid has gifts, or talents, and no two are alike. He was mighty in power, but foresight was his special gift. He was a seer, and spoke of a Guide. It seems that will be me. Of a Protector he gave announcement, which is you, Drom. And he had reverence for a Kindler." His glance fell on Ariane. "That is you, for in the end you must kindle the Light of the world and raise a dead god."

If Ariane felt the weight of that responsibility she gave no sign. But he was getting to know her well, and he guessed she would feel it keenly. It was her very purpose, and that of her entire order since the days of Maramne.

"The old staff," Cadawn continued, "came down to me from Conhain, and from before him into the forgotten history of the druids. These bands though," and he reached out to rest a hand on the iron talismans before him, "are older still."

"They are elvish," Ariane said.

"Indeed. How did you know?"

"I've heard something of how Conhain found them. The priestesses had dealings with him from time to time, yet mostly I can sense their magic. It's different from druid magic. Different from mine too."

"And you, Drom? Have you heard stories about them?"

"Nothing," Drom answered. "Stories of Conhain are frowned upon, at least in the cities where the Court Druids have greater sway. Of the bands, I've heard even less."

Cadawn looked fierce at that. No doubt it reminded him of his enemy.

"The bands are called hathlinden. It is an elvish term. Conhain learned of them in antiquity, in the era of our first king's grandson. It was then that the shadow of evil fell over Camlanta. At that time they were in the hoard of the dragon Rah-essen."

That brought childhood memories back to Drom. "Is it true that the druid's left hand was burned away in dragon fire?"

"It was. Conhain suffered greatly, and life was difficult for him. It was Rah-essen who did that to him, but on his first attempt to obtain the hathlinden. It was not successful. However, his second attempt, some thirty years later, was. He and the warrior Rathglen slew the dragon. The hoard was left where it was near the top of Dragon-fire Peak, and may still be there today for all I know, but likely guarded by a different dragon. They are slow to forget wrongs and swift to find abandoned hoards.

"Anyway, Conhain had obtained the bands and that was all he needed. His thought was only of the future of Camlanta, for he foresaw that the shadow of those times would lengthen as the centuries passed. He knew it was not his part to confront the evil directly. Rather, he laid down a path for those to follow who were ordained to do so. Yet he spoke vaguely for fear of the prophesies being learned and interpreted by the enemy."

"A wise man," Drom said. "And though I have agreed to go on this quest, you know I am not without flaws.

Conhain thought only of Camlanta. I'm not so noble. I go for my own reasons, but I fear what may happen to me."

"Death?" asked the druid. "There is no shame in fearing that."

"No. That is not what I meant."

3. The Tree of Aroth

The silence inside the hut was deep now, equal to the hush of the village until a waterhen gave its piercing cry in the distance.

"What do you fear, if not death?" Cadawn asked.

Drom little liked the idea of talking about himself. Still less his troubles. These two would journey with him though, and he owed them the truth.

"I'm not a good man. My past has shown that, but I've improved since I left the arena. Fighting brings out the worst in me. Brashness. Over-confidence. The thrill of beating an enemy. Arrogance. Unless we're lucky, we'll be forced to confront our enemies, and I fear, more than anything, falling back into my own ways."

There was silence again. Drom felt foolish, yet he could not tell them the full truth, that there were times that he heard the chanting of the arena crowds in his mind, and he loved it, even lusted for it to be real again.

They took him seriously though. They could not know the depth of his feeling on this, though Ariane glanced at him with a searching look, but still they did not dismiss his statement out of hand.

"Matters of the spirit are your province," Cadawn said, gesturing at Ariane. "What do you say?"

She answered without hesitation and looked direct into Drom's eyes.

"I know you now. Not just your legend, spread among the people, and the lies of the king and vizier, spat out like venom. I have searched your mind, if not deeply. You I trust above all others, and if you are imperfect, who among us is different? As Aroth said on a time: *he who proclaims his righteousness stalks as a wolf among sheep. He who acknowledges his faults walks the straight path toward the Kingdom of Light.*"

Drom was shocked. He had not known she thought highly of him. He did not deserve it, and he would do what he could to live up to her expectations. Yet it did not ease his fear. He knew his weaknesses better than she.

He gave no further comment, and Cadawn crossed his arms and sighed.

"It's settled then. We three will go, and alone. It's our best chance. And we'll trust in each other. Fully. None of us is guaranteed of fulfilling our role. Not Guide, nor Protector nor Kindler. All we can do is try our best, and history will record our efforts."

Even the waterhens were silent now, and nothing stirred in the village. Inside the hut it was near dark, and the embers blackened.

Into that silence Ariane almost whispered. "We all have weaknesses. The Dark, through its instruments such as the Court Druids, will test us. A shadow lies over us, as it does over all humanity. Our task is to seek the Light within ourselves even as we seek it in the world."

Cadawn looked thoughtful. "You cannot pass the test if you do not undertake the trial."

It was just words to Drom. He knew there was wisdom there. He knew as well there was a darkness on his spirit. You could not kill before a crowd to entertain them and not have the blood seep into your soul.

When he spoke though, he changed the subject. "If we're to seek a new druid staff as our first quest, where do we go? Do the prophecies tell us? Presumably not just any piece of timber will do?"

He knew the prophesies would not. At least not clearly. He had heard enough stories, or history of Camlanta, to know they were never perfectly clear.

Cadawn took a deep breath. "Indeed not. The forces of magic that flow through a druid's staff are strong. Many timbers would break. Oak is enough for most magic, but not the highest."

"It is true then?" Ariane asked.

The druid raised an eyebrow. "You know what is needed?"

"We have our own lore, handed down from priestess to priestess."

The druid looked at Drom. "This may surprise you. I should have known that the Cult of Aroth would be aware of it, but our enemies likely aren't. We can hope so, anyway. I said just now that a druid staff must be strong to endure the forces of magic. This is a time of great need though. The destiny of the realm is in the balance, and if we fail maybe other lands, one by one until the shadow lies over all Alithoras. So the staff must be more than a conduit of magic. It must lend great power of itself. It must possess its own magic. Can you guess where such timber is to be found?"

It was beyond Drom. He was a warrior, and disliked magic. There was some in his sword, but he did not understand it, nor need to in order to use it. This was a different thing altogether. Even so, he cast his mind over all the stories he had heard. There were forests where the power of faery was said to linger, but he had never heard of a single tree that was in any way special.

Even as he thought that though a stray idea came to his mind. His eyes widened a little.

"It cannot be," he said.

"Ah, you guess," Cadawn answered. "And it's fitting, is it not, given our quest?"

21

"You cannot mean the Tree of Aroth? Not where the god himself was killed."

Cadawn straightened in his chair. "That is what I mean, and though it might seem blasphemous, it is not."

"How could it not be?"

"This is the legend that has come down to me," Cadawn said. "Once Conhain had retrieved the hathlinden, he felt an urgency. Over time, it made itself clear to him. The Tree of Aroth is old. Older than the hills, literally. Some say it was there at the beginning of time. I don't know if that's true, but it predates the Shadowed Wars by far. It's said that it's the oldest living thing in Alithoras, and that Aroth himself called it forth to grow when the world was young."

Drom had heard those stories. It never made sense to him. Aroth had died there, and by some accounts he knew his death was drawing close. Why allow himself to be killed there in a place of such beauty, for such was the reputation of the valley in which the tree grew and more so for the tree itself.

The druid's voice dropped to a whisper. "The story goes that the tree itself spoke to Cadawn, and summoned him. And once there, commanded him to sever a branch as a staff. Two times the tree asked him, and he denied it out of reverence, but then the leaves of the tree whispered to him, and the mournful wind in them was like weeping, and the glimmer of dew upon them as tears. On the third time, he relented. A branch bent itself down, and the tree shivered as he cut the wood."

The druid looked grim, and there was a kind of awe in the glint of his eyes in the near dark.

"It is told that the tree said more. *In the days to come your order will have great need against evil. To make the druids ready for their task, take this thing of power. Forge from it a staff. Join the hathlinden to it. And make other talismans. Hide them. They are*

22

*too strong for normal times. But each in its place will be found by the
appointed person."*

"So the story goes that Conhain fashioned a staff of
great power. Greater than his own. Yet he knew it was not
for him, and he hid it, and there it waits still, ready for a
different druid. Ready for the great battle that must be
fought between Light and Dark. Ready," he said solemnly,
"for us."

4. Farewells

The world seemed asleep while they discussed in the dark hut the events of the distant past. As always though, that past seemed to bubble up all around them.

Drom thought on that a moment. Here they were, in Car Sagoth, a name out of legend. They had walked the land, and seen the Tainglint Mountains, renowned in story and song, and Dragon-fire peak had been visible, if far away. And a gortha of faery had hunted them. The old world was all about him, and for the first time he began to sense how it waited for its time again. The age of humanity dominated now, but there were other things out there, watching for their turn as a cat that stands still while its prey flitters about, getting closer and closer.

"The Cult of Aroth has heard that story," Ariane said. "It is said that the High Priestess during that time was friends with Archdruid Conhain."

Cadawn agreed. "Such is the history that has come down to us to."

Drom was growing tired. He was done talking, but he had one last question.

"I don't suppose either of them left a record where this staff was hidden?"

Cadawn laughed. "If it were so easy, the enemy would be there before us. No, there is no record. Nor do I think Conhain ever told anyone. If he mistrusted them, he would not. If he loved them, still less would he have done so. It would only make them a target for capture and torture until they told what they knew."

"Then how are we supposed to find it?"

The eyes of the druid gleamed in the dark. "This only the prophecy says, handed down from archdruid to archdruid and none other until now. When the time comes the Guide, Protector and Kindler must seek Brandwil's Seat. There magic will reveal to them what they seek."

Brandwil was a name Drom had heard. He was a legend of ancient days.

"He was a great hero, but I've never heard of his *seat*. His throne, maybe?"

"That's possible," the druid answered. "It could mean several things, but most likely it refers to a hill in the south of Camlanta. It was close to many of his battles, and his fortress, and there is a stone bench there, supposedly, that he sat on to view his lands and watch for enemies. Of course, according to the story he was also a giant, and the bench of stone is likewise large."

It was not much to go on. Jumbled stories from long ago, but it was a start.

They took some well-earned rest after that, but at midday two days following the three of them left the village. It was not a quiet affair, but they feared no spies or enemies here.

Drums beat loudly, and there was singing in the village. As they left, a single bonfire was lit just outside the palisade and there were many waves and farewells.

"The bonfire is for luck," Cadawn said. "Fire is sacred to the druids, for it represents the sun."

It was with surprise that Drom realized he was sad to leave this place. He had not thought a swamp could be beautiful, but he was getting to like it. It was a vast area of natural splendor, and in its way just as peaceful as his farm had been. Likewise, the people were different from any that he had known, but unceasingly friendly.

A dread thought occurred to him, and it made him angry too.

"You must have thought of this already, Cadawn. You and your people. If we fail in our quest the power of the vizier and king will increase. By going on it, you're drawing the attention of the enemy upon you. They might have left you alone for centuries, but after this, if they survive, they'll come to exterminate everyone in Car Sagoth. The gortha you took care of, but can you destroy entire armies?"

They passed along a narrow road that took them to a low place in the swamp. Broad swathes of water, stagnant and without current, lay to either side.

"Armies have tried to destroy us in the past, and failed. Even so, you're right. It might take them several years, and their losses will be horrific, but the vizier will come against us if we fail."

A fish leaped in the water nearby with a gleam of silver and a sudden splash. A swamp harrier glided through the air above, and in the distance was the ceaseless call of water hens, and closer some of their kind, if quiet, darted into reeds at the approach of the travelers, tails flicking.

Drom was determined to fulfill his task. He did not want red war to come to this land, or any other part of Camlanta. Even the cities. Yet he was just one small man, and no matter how famed he had been in the old days, he was nothing more than a simple swordsman. He feared the vizier, and with good reason. It was impossible to beat such as he, in the end. The entire strength of the kingdom was his to command, and against that prophesy sent three individuals.

It was a joke. And not one that made him laugh. Even so, he and Ariane had survived so far. Now Cadawn was with them, and his power was great. Was he a match for the vizier? Maybe that was a test that was coming. One to one, it was possible. Against armies though…

He left that thought unfinished. What counted now was stealth. They may only be three, but secrecy was a powerful weapon.

If only they could find the staff, then he would begin to believe that somehow Aroth was not entirely dead. That his power still held some sway in the land, and, here and there, it was able to help them.

Several days passed as they moved slowly through Car Sagoth. Nothing was done at speed in the swamp, and certainly not travel. It was dangerous even with Cadawn, who knew all the secret ways. For outsiders, even experienced in the wilds, it was perilous.

Deadly snakes lay basking on the narrow paths at whiles. At a word from Cadawn, by magic or by noise, they slithered away. Some slipped into the water and glided beneath the surface. Others rustled into tall grasses and lay still.

At night wolves howled, and always that was an eerie sound. Quaint when tucked away in bed with four walls around, but out in the open with the campfire burned down to embers, and in the late stretches of the night, it made the hair on Drom's neck prickle.

It could be silent in Car Sagoth, but mostly it was noisy with the wheeling of huge flocks of ducks overhead, and the chirping of insects and the croaks of frogs both day and night.

They passed through swamp forests where the trees grew stunted and the roots twisted in mire that was neither water nor ground. There were hills, of sorts, bare of anything but tall grasses and the narrow tracks that led to the low crests. From those places they often had a good view, and all over the swamp were columns of smoke rising from villages.

Car Sagoth was more populous than Drom had thought, but Cadawn avoided the villages.

"Every village we stop at will insist on meeting you both," he said. "And giving us a feast. It will slow us down too much. While I recovered, you can be sure our enemies were at work. They must surely know, or guess, who you two are now, for they have their own prophesies."

At length they came to the outer hinterland of the swamp. It was still wet, sometimes even with large bodies of open water, but the paths were wider and the ground firmer. More often than not it sloped upward now too.

It was then they walked past burial mounds again, just as they had coming into the swamp the first time. Some were relatively small, others stretched out to the edge of sight.

Drom studied them grimly. The enemy had tried hard to destroy the true druids, especially deep in the past. They had learned with bitterness the folly of that. Yet if their power grew a little, and the vizier and king were roused as now they must be, not even the dangers of the swamp and great magic would stop them conquering Car Sagoth and the druids, even if at great cost.

They slept that night on a high point, with a small fire near the base of a few stunted oaks that would give them some protection should it rain. Dark clouds rolled overhead and blotted out most of the stars, but no more than a few large drops fell.

All of them slept. They kept no watch, for they feared no attack while still within the borders of the swamp. Tomorrow though, Cadawn told them, they would leave Car Sagoth behind.

Drom dreamed, and his sleep was restless. Always he sought peace. He had found it at his farm, but that was taken from him. To his surprise, he found it here in the swamp as well. It was a place that he could come to love, and maybe already did.

He feared the outside world though. He was Drom, but Isarn the Invincible was his shadow, and he could never leave it behind. In the outside world he would be forced to fight, and the shadow might rise to take over the man.

5. A Warning

They traveled swiftly the next morning. The way forward was easier, for water was giving way to firmer ground, and though the paths were still narrow, they were easy to follow.

Strangely, the path now led a little downward. They entered a canyon of sorts, with rocky cliff faces to either side. These widened away from them as they pressed ahead, and the ground became dangerous again.

Drom, leading his horse, stumbled on a twisted root, and Cadawn reached out to steady him. His grip was firm, but then he released it, took hold of a fallen branch and pressed the point into the ground.

The stick sunk deep in a matter of moments, and Cadawn let it go.

"Be wary still," the druid said. "We are nearly out of the swamp, but not quite."

They moved ahead, and Cadawn still did so quickly. The other two were careful to tread in his exact path.

At mid-morning there was a sudden rush of wings. Seven swans, gleaming black against the dark blue of the river of daylight that ran above them, sped by, red bills thrust out before them.

Cadawn paused. It was dark in the canyon, the walls to either side blocking out much of the sunlight. It was well treed too, but often there were thick growths of ferns, some like trees themselves.

"What is it?" Ariane asked.

"I don't know. Swans are said to be the messengers of the gods. And black signifies evil and red danger."

"Or maybe they were just swans," Drom said. He had traveled widely, and seen them in many colors before. Though in truth, never quite like that.

Cadawn shrugged, and then picked his way forward over a little brook. It was only a handspan deep, and rocks had been placed at regular intervals to ease the crossing, though they were slippery.

The path wound steeply downward, and it grew darker still. Druids, supposedly, could read the omens of nature. Drom began to feel the swans might really have signified something, for this place had an ill feeling to it.

"Look," Ariane said, pointing.

Drom followed her gesture and saw nothing at first. Then looking a little higher along the steep cliffs he saw what she meant. Great figures were carved into the stone. Age had worn them down. Rain, wind and heat had eroded and cracked them. Yet still there was a sense of majesty about them.

"Druid work?" Drom asked.

"No. Druids prefer to work with wood. There were people in Car Sagoth before us, though they were mere legend even before we first came."

The carvings reminded Drom of those he and Ariane had seen in the mountain pass when they had fled his farm. There was a history to Camlanta that most had forgotten, and even the druids whose knowledge ran deep by comparison barely scratched the surface. One day even Isarn the Invincible would be forgotten, and the quest they now went on.

Not far ahead the trail led to a small cave. It was little more than a hollowing out of the cliff face, yet it would offer shelter from rain. Inside was a different kind of art, and much more recent. Seven figures were painted in ochre on the stone, and on the floor beneath each was a small slab, marked with strange signs.

Drom could not read the writing, but he knew the likenesses of the gods when he saw them.

"It's a chapel," Cadawn said. "There are several like this in the swamp, but this is the best preserved."

"Not just a chapel," Ariane answered. "But an old one. This is from a time before Aroth became incarnate. See there?" She pointed at the figure of a woman riding a racing horse. "That's Ebona, who alone of the gods left the land of her birth."

It was not an image depicted very often. So far as Drom could recall he had seen it only once, and that was in a book in the vizier's palace. He had learned much in the archdruid's library, and more from the archdruid himself. Those were different times, and it shamed him to think that once he had been friends with that man and the king. Even so, he had learned much that others could not even guess.

Those memories took him back to the arena. When he was not fighting, or training to fight, which took up much more time, he often read in his small room beneath the stands. Once it became known that he did so, and had an insatiable appetite for books, merchants and lords and even druids brought him material from all across the realm, and beyond, to try to curry his favor. And he rewarded them by attending their parties and entertaining their guests with accounts of his fights.

Ariane took a few moments to stop and pray. Cadawn joined her, and Drom, feeling uncomfortable, moved away. He studied the cliff face some more, and marked that it was dark enough in the canyon, at least in this spot, to see the stars in daylight hours.

Soon the others rejoined him. Ariane seemed serene, but Cadawn's expression had been slightly troubled since seeing the swans, and praying had done nothing to change that.

They moved ahead. The path led upward now, and the ravine widened again. The stars disappeared as it grew brighter, and they began to climb a long slope that was mostly rock.

It was a hard climb, and the horses labored. By its end the ravine was gone, and they had crested a hill. Here, they were on the edge of the swamp. Behind lay Car Sagoth, but every step forward was into the rest of Camlanta. It spread out before them in rolling downlands.

A single tree marked the spot. It was a hawthorn, but not stunted like the oaks of the swamp. And beneath it something moved.

A group of crows fluttered, or so Drom thought. Then he realized instead that it was a black cloak moving strangely in the breeze, and a figure now pulled it tight and walked toward them.

Whoever it was seemed tall, even for a man. Yet it was no man. It was a woman, and Drom looked at her suspiciously.

Cadawn stiffened. "What do you wish here, creature of faery?"

The figure came closer, then stopped. Whoever it was did not seem to wish them harm, but the look on her face was not liking either. She pulled back her hood, and her raven black hair spilled out in sharp contrast to the milk-white skin of her face.

"You know me, druid."

"I know you, Morrigan. Of faery you are, ancient even among your kind. What do you wish here?"

Drom felt the hair stand on the back of his neck, but he did not draw his blade. She stood as a warrior herself, and he saw now the slim blade belted at her waist, but she had not drawn it.

"I would see the Guide, Protector and Kindler with my own eyes."

33

"You know who we are?"

Her gaze fell on them all, one by one, and her eyes were as dark pits full of shadows. Even so, Drom sensed no evil. This was a being beyond the Light and the Dark. Something that existed independently. According to stories she could be a terrible foe or a great friend.

"You have seen us," Cadawn answered. "More to the point, what are you going to do now?"

She smiled at him, and her teeth were white above her sharp yet graceful nose.

"You have long been foretold, and some of my kind wish you dead. Others look more favorably at you."

"And you?"

"I have not decided."

Drom knew there were those in the arena who treated her like a god and prayed to her. She was a warrioress, and associated with battle. He dismounted and bowed low.

"Many a warrior offers prayers to you," he said.

"But not you."

"No. I trust rather to my strength and skill. The tales say you choose your friends and your enemies wisely. Yet no tale tells of your beauty. I fear humanity has forgotten much that our ancestors must have known better."

She turned her gaze on him, and those dark eyes fixed him as though they were daggers.

"Pretty words, mortal. Do you mean them, or do you try to flatter for your benefit?"

Drom grinned at her. "I'm not afraid to die. I speak the truth because it's what I feel. You know I'm a warrior, and I know you're the Queen of Battles. You can search my mind for the truth, can you not?"

She studied him a moment. "No. You're not afraid to die. You have other fears though. Still, you speak the truth, or so I deem."

The Morrigan drew herself up and glanced at them all again, her eyes veiled now. With a slim hand, white as snow, she covered her black hair again with her hood.

"This I will say, for the powers of the old world move again. Your enemies will invoke ancient magic, and as a counter to that, I am permitted to give you aid. Should I choose. And because of your bold words, I do."

The sun had begun to fall and afternoon was wearing on. The Morrigan cast a dark shadow in the angled light, and suddenly she seemed otherworldly.

"Beware the Court Druids. They grow desperate. The world spins and destiny unravels, and certain as they have been for a thousand years to weave fate to their choosing, the threads now outpace them and they fumble. That makes them ready to risk magics that have no place in mortal hands. One will come against you that is druid, and yet more than druid. The talisman he carries is not his by right. Remember that. And another will come sooner and surprise will be his ally. Expect nothing, and you will not be surprised."

She finished speaking, and stepped back. Drom offered a bow, and Cadawn and Ariane followed. Then the Morrigan turned, her robes spinning and the shadow she cast twisting.

All in one motion, woman, cloak and shadow coalesced, and then with a loud caw a crow flapped its wings where she had been and glided away swiftly out of sight.

Cadawn whistled. "Well, that could have been much worse. She is one that might easily have fought us, and that would've been a disaster." He looked at Drom questioningly. "How did you know the way to speak to her? Our lives hung upon a thread until you did."

Drom glanced at Ariane, and then looked away, muttering.

"I know women. Be they gods or creatures of faery. And I know warriors too. Neither are hard to speak to if you have the knack. Lucky for us I do."

He did not look at Ariane, but he felt her gaze upon him.

6. I Have Failed

Amrog could sense the gortha at all times. The magic of summoning still connected them, and though they could not communicate he felt in a vague way what it thought.

And it lusted for blood. It was famished for the taste of human flesh that it had not devoured in centuries. The long slumber was over, and it needed food to give it strength, and none would do save the prey it had been sent to hunt.

With anticipation the druid realized the creature was getting close. He felt the rush of its speed as it pursued the enemy in the last flight. His own blood rushed through him, and he breathed swiftly while his heart raced.

Then he felt shock, and he did not know what it meant. Shock turned to fear, and he cried out himself regardless of the soldiers that were about him. They turned their gazes to him, and he cringed at being seen to be vulnerable. He could not stop the rush of feelings though, and they were so real they could be his own. At the last, he went down on his knees and screamed as the gortha died.

He could not believe it. How had it been done? He did not know, but he tasted death in his mouth and his veins ran cold with fear.

Mastering himself, he stood. "The gortha is dead," he whispered. "Our enemies live. Hasten forward, and death to the man who holds back."

It was all he could think of to retake command of the men. They rode at a gallop now, and it might be that they would forget his momentary weakness if they were occupied.

He would not though. It was his second shock. The death of the gortha was bad enough, but to be outmaneuvered by his enemy, even if he did not know how, was galling beyond endurance.

His mount raced ahead, and he thought as he rode. It was not hard to piece things together. Isarn and the girl were near to Car Sagoth. Perhaps they had killed the gortha, but more likely they had help. If so, that likely came from the swamp druids.

Magic had been used. Strong magic. Perhaps stronger than he possessed himself, and that gave him pause for thought.

It might be just as well that he would not catch up to them before they entered the swamp. The soldiers did not need to know that. Racing ahead gave them something else to think about instead of his weakness. It also gave him time to plan. The hunt was not yet finished. He could not follow into the swamp, and he must tell the archdruid of his failure. Yet the archdruid was resourceful and would offer advice, knowledge or the help of more druids.

They came to the site of the battle a little after dawn. The storm had receded far away, but the grass remained wet. Traces of magic still scented the air, at least for those such as a druid who could sense them.

Amrog raised a hand, and the column halted. If they went ahead they would leave marks everywhere, and though he knew the gortha had died, he did not know how.

"Catagern!" he called.

The farmer nudged his mount forward. He was reluctant to serve, and yet he had more skill and courage than the soldiers. Most of all, his ability as a tracker was excellent.

"The gortha died near here. That I know, but little more. Unravel this riddle for me, if rain has not washed all marks away."

Without a word the farmer dismounted and handed his reins to a soldier. Then he picked his way forward over the ground, swift at first and then slower.

Catagern took his time. Sometimes he bent low and studied a mark, then like a hound on a scent he strode quickly until he came to some other mark of interest. When he finally returned, his face was grim.

"As you say, the gortha died nearby. It was over there," and he pointed to a spot that looked like any other to Amrog. "The creature perished by flame. It was hot enough to melt stone, but the druid stood way over there." Again he pointed to some place that looked like everywhere else.

"That is all you discovered?"

"No. The druid was wounded first, probably cut by a blade. But before he could be killed an army intervened. They came from the mounds, and went back into them. Nor, I think, did the druid kill the gortha. Its eventual death was too far away. The flame, I think, came from above."

Even as he spoke the farmer made the sign against evil.

"You're saying the gortha was killed by ghosts, and that one of them flew?"

"It's not me saying that. It's what the marks show, plain as day for anyone who can read them."

Amrog was about to laugh, and then he remembered Car Sagoth was often called a land of mists and ghosts in the old lore. Armies had been destroyed by the risen dead, so the stories went. And even the vizier had said at times that the rebel druids had magic like to their own, but different. That their powers were great, at least in the swamp.

39

His mind reached out to other lore then. Dragons. Once there had been many in the land, until the Shadowed Wars. Even they had been killed in those cataclysms.

Carefully, he studied the barrows. They were old, and he had seen their like before. The dead of those ancient battles were under them, and who was to say that a dragon was not, as well?

"Good work," he said grudgingly. The farmer seemed neither pleased nor displeased, which was yet another difference to the soldiers. They fawned for his compliments.

A sense of awe was gradually flowing over Amrog. The swamp druids were *strong*, and they had command of great magic. With it came a sense of destiny. Right now, it was in flux. The eternal battle between Dark and Light was playing out around him, and he was part of it. His role was to champion the Dark.

But how?

It was a vexing question. It was clear he could not enter the swamp. He was one druid with a small force. Armies had perished making such an attempt.

"What now?" a soldier asked.

Amrog looked at him bleakly. "We cannot enter Car Sagoth."

"Then we should return home," the farmer said, stepping closer. By that he meant he wanted to return to his own easy life, and Amrog did not like it. Too long such as he had lived off the fat of the land while druids and soldiers risked their lives for the advancement of their cause.

The soldiers though had a better attitude. "Let's test those swamp dwellers," one said.

"They're only rebels," another one offered. "We should kill them all."

Amrog liked their attitude, but their brains were in their horses' manure. They had listened to the propaganda back in the capital, and actually believed it. Fools.

Yet again, the farmer showed he was smarter than they, even if not loyal to the cause.

"They killed a gortha. Now they'll have even more help. To go into the swamp is to commit suicide."

He was right. Even so, Amrog eyed him coldly. "Our task is not done."

"The only task we can accomplish by going in is to die."

He was bold. That was certain. No soldier would say that to a druid, no matter if it were right or wrong.

Amrog made a quick decision. "We cannot enter, but our task isn't done. We'll set up camp a mile back the way we came, and I'll think on what's to be done next. It will *not* be returning home."

The camp was established quickly. Amrog did not think they were in danger. There were few stories of the rebel druids venturing beyond their borders, though they must do so at times even if in secret. Either way, he set a watch.

While the men worked, he pondered his situation. He had failed. There was no other interpretation of events. It did not matter that his quarry had help from the druids. They should not have reached close enough to Car Sagoth that such a thing could happen.

Equally, the archdruid was intolerant of errors. All the more so now, given that Drom had at long last been located and an accursed High Priestess discovered. And yet he must report what had happened. First, so as not to look like he was trying to conceal his failure, and second, to get information or aid that would help him fulfil his mission.

41

He was not sure that anything could be done except to instigate a war against Car Sagoth. But he did not possess the full facts as did the archdruid. If something else could be done, despite his failure, it might still be by him, and he would therefore have opportunity to redeem himself.

There was no deceiving the archdruid. Nothing could be done but admit his failure, and hope.

The camp was established, and the afternoon drew on. Amrog gave instructions that anyone who slept on watch would be executed, and that he was leaving camp now and would test their vigilance later.

If they were attacked from the swamp and his men perished, it would also mean Amrog's own death. The archdruid would not tolerate two failures in a row.

Walking calmed him, but as dusk fell he found a hollow surrounded by shrubs, and a stunted tree, long since fallen in some storm or through age, and suitable for his purpose.

There was no point delaying things. He summoned his magic and sent tendrils of fire to wrap around the dry trunk. It did not take long before the timber began to burn, and then he let it be. He did not need the fire to communicate with the archdruid, yet it made things easier. Fire was not one of the elements, and being neither earth, air nor water had properties of magic. That assisted him, even if not necessary.

When the flames began to roar, he added more magic, and of a different kind. His spirit became one with the fire, and then as it leaped and twisted he rode the currents into the air and shot like an arrow from a bow to the capital, and to the archdruid's quarters. At this time of day he was always alone, ready to talk to druids across the realm, or else reading of the druids collection of lore books.

The archdruid was aware of him instantly.

"Approach," he said.

Amrog swept down, a spirit form that flickered like the fire. Most would not detect him, but some, even not trained in magic, would sense and perhaps see him.

"Report."

Amrog told of the chase with brevity. He spoke of the gortha, and his sensing of its destruction. Lastly, he told of the battle on the borders of the swamp, and what the tracker had identified and his guess as to the necromancy spell for soldiers. And at least one dragon.

All the while the archdruid remained silent, and only at mention of dragons did his expression change. Amrog feared it would be taken as an exaggeration to somehow excuse his failure, and he had dreaded saying it. Yet that was what the facts pointed to, and to say less was to invite trouble as well.

"You have failed me."

"Yes, my lord." He offered no excuse. It was better for the archdruid to decide the extent of failure than to try to persuade him it had not occurred.

"You have also told the truth, and some would not have."

That surprised Amrog. He had expected to have to defend his comment about dragons, if nothing else.

With a gesture the archdruid indicated the books in his room.

"There is much lore here. Some books are only for the archdruid. There is a record of dragons in ancient history. We know some died around Car Sagoth in the Shadowed Wars, and we know, or at least I do, that the rebels have raised them against us in the past."

Amrog felt a rush of relief, yet it was premature.

"It is well for you that you told the truth. If not, you would be dead by now. Even so, you still failed, and that requires severe punishment."

"Yes, my lord."

"Have you anything else to say?"

"Only this, but it is a mere guess. I cannot be certain."

"Speak."

Amrog repeated what the tracker had told him. "The druid was injured by the gortha. There was a little blood, indicating he had been struck by a blade, and the blades of a gortha are poisonous, as you know. It is possible the false archdruid is dead or dying."

"And?"

That was a shock to Amrog. He wondered, and not for the first time, if the archdruid could read his thoughts.

"I sensed a different magic. It was the unraveling of an ancient spell, and I sensed an elvish quality to it. I cannot be sure, but I suspect the Druid Staff was broken in the encounter with the gortha."

The eyes of the archdruid widened a fraction. It was only a slight change of expression, and instantly gone, but on the face of the archdruid, who was never surprised by anything, it was the equivalent of complete shock.

"Well, that is interesting."

There was silence for a moment. Amrog waited to see what the archdruid would make of it all, and what punishment would be delivered.

"Well do I believe your tale, though you feared otherwise. And just as well you spoke truth. There is a prophecy, not committed to any book, but handed down from archdruid to archdruid. Only once was that chain broken. It required the new druid to summon the spirit of the dead druid to reforge it."

The vizier began to pace. It was a sign of intense thought, and the skin around the empty eye-socket wrinkled.

"It can be said now, for you must know, and the others. The time is upon us. According to the prophecy, when the staff of the rebel archdruid breaks, dragons will burn the skies once more. A new staff will be needed, and the Rebel, the Slave and the Heretic will seek it."

Amrog understood at once. Both who these people were, and what it meant. The time was come when Aroth would be resurrected, if he even existed. Certainly the enemy would try. Either way, they must be stopped lest they rouse the people of the kingdom.

The archdruid sat. Whatever he had been considering, his decisions were made.

"You have failed me, Amrog."

Amrog felt the power of his spell subside, and the pull back to his body begin. Yet still he waited.

"You have a rare chance at redemption though. I will send other aid, for this is greater by far than I thought, and already I thought it important. Not least for personal revenge."

The archdruid rubbed his empty eye-socket, and continued.

"They must not live. Ordering you to enter the swamp, though a suitable punishment for your failure, would only lead to your death. However, those whom you seek must leave it."

"Does the prophecy say where they'll search for the staff?"

"No. But it must be to the south. There was more to the prophecy, and while no location was specified, it suggested the enemy will fly as an arrow on a south wind over a battlement of dead men."

Amrog felt the pull to his body strengthen. With it now came pain. If he did not return soon, he would die. Not for long could the body endure without the spirit, or at least not his. He had not fully mastered the magic yet.

"Travel swiftly. Skirt the swamp, and go near the Tainglint Mountains where they diminish into rolling hills at the south of Car Sagoth. There bide your time and wait at that higher vantage where you can see abroad. I cannot be sure, but there I think those whom you pursue will come to you. The Dark and the Light always try to be in balance. After that, it is up to you. Nevertheless, do not fail again."

It was good advice, and the archdruid might know more than he said as well. Amrog was troubled though.

"The rebel druids are strong. I am but one, and only have a small company with me. May I ask for more help?"

There was a cold silence. Then the archdruid nodded.

"You ask, and you will receive. It is unlikely any druids or soldiers I send to you will reach you in time, so I shall offer you aid of a different sort. The leader of the rebels is Cadawn. Of him, you must be careful. Do not underestimate him. Know that his power is great. Yet I shall enhance yours. Brace yourself, druid."

Instantly, Amrog felt the magic. It was of a kind he had not seen before, but that was possible. High in the order as he was, the archdruid kept many secrets to himself. Here and there he might dole this out to one, or that to another. Mostly, it was only at the end of an archdruid's life that he chose his successor and taught them all the highest mysteries. And if there was insufficient time, necromancy had been invoked more than once, according to rumor.

With a rush, he felt power flow into him. This was similar to the rites used to prolong the life of the king, yet different. Strength coursed through him, and his senses sharpened. His own magic seemed to boil within him, seeking an outlet. He crushed it down. It would have an outlet soon when he met this other druid, and now he felt strong enough to defeat him. Strong enough to take on all the druids in Car Sagoth by himself.

With a gesture, the archdruid dismissed him. Despite his new power, he was as a leaf floating on the surface of a river.

He came back to his own body, cold and shuddering. He had been near death. Yet he had lived, and even been enhanced. Nor had he been punished. His luck was riding high.

Even so, something about this new magic within him did not feel right.

7. He Will Still Hunt Us

The sun lowered in the west, yet there was still time to ride forward.

"We leave Car Sagoth now," Cadawn said. "Dangers will beset us, and tests lie ahead. Keep your eyes open."

The words matched what Drom was thinking, and he voiced his concern.

"The gortha was slain, but not the druid who summoned it. He is out there somewhere, and his kind do not give up easily."

Ariane sat taller in her saddle and spoke softly. "Aroth is with us. He will protect us, while we are worthy."

Drom was not so sure of that. He trusted little in the powers of a dead god, and it seemed Cadawn agreed with him.

"I have my own protection, of a kind," the druid said. He reached into his saddle bags and withdrew the hathlinden. They seemed dull and lifeless, yet as the westering sun caught them they gleamed with sudden color.

The druid slipped his hands into them, and they molded into a new shape even as Drom watched. The metal became as water, then froze again as armbands about his wrists.

Drom could not believe it, yet he had seen it with his own eyes.

Cadawn winked at him. "The strength of our enemies is great, but we have power too. Now let us ride!"

The druid kicked his horse into a gallop, and Drom and Ariane followed. There was no path, but the land was mostly grassed with a few trees. It was a good place to ride, and they would have an hour or so to cover as much distance as they could. In the swamp, careful travel mattered. Out here, speed would serve them best.

The horses thundered forward, and Drom liked it. He was no great rider, but few could ride a horse at speed and not feel the majesty of the animal.

He glanced at Ariane. She rode with great skill, and her horse was good. He did not doubt she could outpace both he and the druid, or ride terrain at speed that would cause them to halt. Yet she stayed with them, a smile on her face.

Beyond her Drom saw the trailing end of the Tainglint Mountains where the great chain of peaks faltered into ancient hills. A darkness was over them, for the sun lay behind. Yet their forest-shrouded ridges looked out like dark eyes onto the lower lands below. Drom felt uneasy, and he did not know why.

As the light failed they set up a camp. Cadawn, as always, found a good place. A small brook babbled nearby, and trees surrounded a little dell, so both earth and plants offered protection against weather.

The land changed little as they traveled. The difference between here and the swamp was not great in terms of height, but it was enough to ensure dry ground, rolling slopes and clusters of trees.

It was not an inhabited land though. This was the far edge of the realm, and most people dwelt along the western coastline.

They saw no fires as they passed through the wild country like ghosts. There were no herds nor fences nor villages. Even so, they moved with stealth, preferring to use the small woods and low lying paths to hide them from the higher ground to the west.

Despite their care, they made good time. Cadawn was in a hurry, for he knew as well as Drom that the enemy druid was still out there, and other help could be arriving to bolster him.

It was pointless to try to guess what form that would take. Soldiers, druids or magic were all possible. All Drom needed to know was that the vizier would do something. His druid had failed once, and if there was anything Castanuin hated it was being outmaneuvered. It was intolerable to him, and lately it had happened multiple times. Ever since Ariane had come to Drom's farm, the vizier had been stymied. All the more reason that he would be unpredictable, but forceful, in his next action.

They came to the crest of a long slope. It was bare of trees, and there was nowhere to ride that made them less visible. The mountains had faded from sight, and even the diminishing hills at the tail end of the range were barely higher than here. They were smudged with distant trees though, and Drom felt vulnerable.

"Have you been this way before?" Drom asked the druid.

"Not really. We leave the swamp from time to time and travel the land, but mostly we go westward where there are people. What lies ahead of us was once populous, but not since the Shadowed Wars."

A thick mist rolled down from the hills later that day. Summer had started, but the mist was cold and clingy. Yet after they had set camp and eaten, a wind rose and blew the fog away. The night grew clear again, and the stars twinkled in the sky.

"Tell me this, Cadawn," Drom spoke up when the flames of the campfire began to die down. "What are the stars?"

"They are suns, Drom, just like our own. Yet very far away. Some burn much brighter than ours, yet they are so far sway we cannot see them. And around them spin other worlds. Some, even like our own."

It was not the answer he had heard as a child, but it was the same answer to the same question that Castanuin had given him long ago. Court Druids and their rebel brethren remained similar in many ways. But they were different in the ways that counted most.

"I've been thinking about your sword," Cadawn said unexpectedly. "Since we first met actually."

"What about it?"

"Let's just say I have a theory. I cannot prove it yet though. May I see it?"

Warriors did not like others handling their weapons much, but Cadawn was now a friend. Drom stood, and drew the blade with a slow whisper from its sheath.

"It's a sword fit for a king. Castanuin little liked the king giving it to me."

He handed the blade, hilt first, to the druid. And the druid took it almost reverently.

A long while Cadawn held the sword, tracing his fingers over the metal blade and the wooden hilt. He did not show the surprise that Ariane had when she first touched it, but his look of concentration was intense.

Ariane gazed keenly too, looking to Cadawn for his reaction. Without doubt she had spoken to the druid about it, and now he tested it to try to discern its properties.

Cadawn hesitated, and then with a quick gesture rapped the flat of the blade against the hathlinden on his arm. A bell-like sound pealed forth with a flash of silver light. Strange runes suddenly glowed upon the arm braces, and to Drom's surprise upon the blade of his sword too. He had never seen them before.

The letters faded quickly, but the bell-like note seemed to linger on the edge of hearing. It was a sweet sound, full of beauty but tinged with sadness.

Cadawn handed the blade back. "Fit for a king, you say? It's more than that. An emperor could carry that sword and feel unworthy. It's of elven make, and not of any common forging even for them. The hilt, as Ariane told me, is different. There's power there too, but of a kind I haven't felt before. It's remote. Dormant even. I don't think you have yet plumbed the depths of the magic within, but you have not been fully assaulted by the Dark yet."

It was nothing new. It seemed not even the druid fully understood the weapon, and maybe no one did. Drom smiled, thinking of the chagrin of Castanuin when he learned of the gift, for certainly the archdruid had sensed as much as Cadawn had.

With a flourish, Drom threw the blade upward so that it spun in the air, and as it dropped he caught it by the hilt.

"I like the magic in it. More than once it's saved me, but it's still just a sword and of little use unless the arm that wields it has skill. It's time for me to do a little practice."

He walked out of the camp and into the dark, but he heard Cadawn speak softly.

"And the heart has courage that guides the arm."

He was not sure if the words were meant for him or for Ariane.

Outside the little dell he found a flat spot of ground. As he usually did when time permitted, he practiced the art of killing.

First it was with the sword. He went through an array of techniques, drilling them individually and correcting his posture as he did so. Many were regular tactics from the arena, but not all.

Some he had learned from his Cheng friend, and these often did not rely on strength but instead honed pliability, deflection, and outright sneakiness.

They had proved useful. He was strong, and even more so in those days. Yet there was always someone stronger. Relying on physical superiority was moronic, even if most warriors did. For him, his eyes had been opened. And the tactics had killed some who thought themselves invulnerable.

It was hard work. Sweat soon dripped from him, but he walked the line, practicing the techniques over and again, in advance and in retreat.

Then he leaped into a sword form, and the elven blade whispered death in the dark air. Then he practiced another, and another. He knew too many to practice all at once. He rotated their training over days. Yet each form served a purpose, taught a skill, and exemplified a strategy.

A breeze cooled the sweat on him. He luxuriated in it for a minute, then put the sword down and followed the same procedure with hand techniques. One at a time he went, trying to perfect his posture and the chain of power from legs to waist to arms.

As before, he then turned to forms. When he was done, sweat dripped from him again and his arms were tired and his legs, particularly his left knee, began to ache.

It did not matter. Training was life in the arena, and laziness was death. He went to the ground, practicing a few rolls and ground-fighting techniques, and then started to do pushups.

They were not the ordinary sort. Again, taught to him by his Cheng friend, these kept the elbows close together and the body rocked down and forward, then back and upward. They were many times harder, and his arms soon trembled and gave way.

He jumped to a branch of nearby tree, and pulled himself up and down until he could do so no more.

It hurt. It all hurt. He was tired of it, but he would do the same tomorrow night. His life depended on recapturing his skills of old.

And so did Ariane's.

8. In Our Power

Drom slept almost immediately on returning to the camp.

The fire had burned low, and they would not feed it much during the night as a precaution. It was impossible to see into the dell, and with the surrounding trees there would be little smoke to see or scent. It was better to be safe though.

They set no watch, and though fearing the druid had not given up on them, it was hard to reason a way he could discover their location, especially so soon after leaving the swamp.

Unless the Court Druids had their own prophesies. It was a thought that haunted Drom's sleep. What if the enemy knew where they were going? Then they could set an ambush.

Despite those thoughts that returned to him several times as sleep rose toward wakefulness, he drifted back into slumber each time.

The dreams came thick and fast. Soon he was in the arena again, and it was a nightmare that he often had. He had won his fight, but then the king called forth another competitor against him. And another. So it went until the sand was red with blood and the crowd roared his name.

It was a battle without end. The king would keep sending opponents at him, and sooner or later he would make a mistake. And the vizier watched it all, his empty eye red and angry, the other eye like a dagger, and a cold smile on his cruel face.

Vaceran! Drom cried in his sleep, but it seemed as a whisper and he could not yell. Even so, in his dreams he could move freely. Other warriors had told him that they could barely move in their dream fights, but that seemed strange to him. Maybe he was different.

Many times he cried out vaceran, and the last time seemed louder. By the power of that word, or his will behind it, or by some strange chance of dreams, the arena fell away.

There was peace now, and dark. Yet the dark slowly receded and was replaced by a thick fog. It was impenetrable, yet it seemed to glimmer with a light of silver.

He did not like the fog. It was better than the arena, yet he still sensed danger. He backed away, and found that he stood upon a hill. Stepping in any direction he began to move downward, and the fog was thicker there, so he stayed where he was.

It was chill, and his mind seemed half awake. He knew he was dreaming, yet he could think too, even if in a dull fashion. Again, other warriors had told him it was not so with them.

A whisper came to him. No. It was the sound of dripping water. Looking to his left he saw three stones in the mist, now suddenly clearer. The grass around them was short and green, but they were ancient things, each leaning in a different direction.

If this were a dream, it was different even for Drom. But at least it was not the arena.

The stones shuddered, and from behind them, or maybe from within them, three figures stepped. One was young and beautiful, and Drom was immediately wary. Another was ageless as the noontide sun, neither young nor old. The other was a hideous crone, yet her Drom trusted most.

"Where am I?" he asked. He knew by instinct that this dream was theirs, created and controlled by them, and not a dream at all but a manifestation of magic.

"In our power," the youngest of them answered.

"I don't think so. In your dream, yes. In your power? Never."

"Beware your pride," the ageless one said. "It has been the downfall of many, not least the kings of Camlanta."

"I'm no king. Pride moves me no more than your average man. It's not my flaw, and you know it. For you are the Three Fates of faery, are you not?"

The women looked at him and said nothing, yet he sensed they spoke one to the other in their minds.

"You are smarter than the king," the eldest of them said at length. "Yet you are still in our power, and defenseless." As she spoke she raised her arm and lightning flashed upward into the sky.

Drom gave answer, and he used it to give himself time to think.

"The king is not as witless as he seems. Evil, yes. But witless, no. Tell me if I'm wrong."

This was a dream, and he knew it. He had seen the lightning, but there was no thunder. Whatever was happening, his body was back in the dell beside the near-dead fire, safe and secure. This was a realm of the mind, and if that were so, anything was possible.

"He thinks he is smart. Perhaps he is just mad though. Perhaps you are?"

Drom laughed. "I'm neither mad nor defenseless. Nor in your power. See!"

Even as he spoke he thought of his sword. He knew how it felt in his hand, the balance of the blade and the magic in it that he often sensed but did not have the skill to fully control.

He thought of it, and raised his hand aloft, and the sword was in his grasp gleaming in the silvery mist-light. A cold flame flickered along the edge of the blade, and then faded.

The three women bowed. "See how fast he learns," said the eldest.

With a nod, the ageless one spoke next. "He is worthy."

"And yet he may still fail," said the youngest.

"Fail what?" Drom asked.

It was a mistake. By asking a question he was playing their game by their own rules. Nevertheless, he was more curious now than anything. Had they wished him harm they would have tried some attack by now.

"We know your quest," the eldest said. Her face was haggard and her wispy gray hair matted and unkempt. Even so, it was her he liked most. He sensed in her no animosity. Of the others, he was less sure.

"It is a task of high order you seek to perform. But know that even gods can die, and that living they may be different from what you expect."

"No doubt. I have other reasons too. If you seek to dissuade me, don't waste your time."

"Ah," the ageless one said. "You protect the girl. Do you wish to know if she is your daughter?"

"I do. But I don't trust any answer you might give, so spare me that. Tell me what you want, and then let me sleep again."

All three of them laughed.

"He is prickly," one said.

"He is wise," another answered.

"He is as he was forged in the arena," the third added.

All around them the mist swirled, and the drip of water from the stones was loud.

"We do not seek to persuade or dissuade," the eldest said after a pause. "The fate of men is nothing to us. We just observe and record. Yet beware! There are worse things in life than failing. If you persist, you may discover that."

"I don't scare easy."

"That we long have known, and all the more so lately. Perhaps you *should* be scared though. Dark things will come against you. There are some within faery who wish your death. A few that might help you, and most are indifferent. How shall you know one from the other?"

"Let's start with you," Drom said. "Do you mean me harm? I say not. If you did, I would kill you. So will I deal with all I meet."

"We are harder to kill than even you," the eldest said. "So fear us not. We merely wished to meet you, for in the web of destiny your thread is longer than most."

"And we wished to see if Aroth chose wisely," the youngest said.

"And did he?"

"Wisdom is a many-edged sword," the ageless one replied. "Should you live long enough, you will discover that."

The eldest took a step forward. "We have seen what we needed to," she said. "Sleep! Forget! Your fate is not yet determined. Let dreams wash over you, and when you wake you will remember nothing of this hill, the standing stones or we three sisters. Forget!"

The mist rose up at her words, and covered the hill like billowing clouds. Drom fell back into darkness, and a great drowsiness took him. Into a deep sleep he fell, beyond slumber and dreams, and when he woke it was dawn.

He felt refreshed. He knew he had experienced nightmares, as he usually did, but he could recall nothing.

And they had been only in the first part of his sleep. The second, closer to his waking, had been that peaceful sleep that healed all sickness of mind and body.

And yet he knew it had not been dreamless either. Something had happened, but what? And then he began to tremble.

9. Evil is at Hand

Drom remembered all he had been told to forget.

Had it been a dream? If so, then there was no reason not to remember. Yet he knew it was real. In a dream it might have happened, but he was awake in it, and those three women were present.

The sun was rising, and Ariane and Cadawn were sitting by the fire, feeding a little tinder to it, and getting ready to heat breakfast.

"You slept long," Ariane said.

"I do not think I slept at all."

He told them of what had happened, and Cadawn questioned him at several points.

"Do you believe me?" Drom asked.

The druid took his time to answer. "You believe it, and that convinces me. That, and the three standing stones. For in the lore of the druids the sidhe in which they dwell is thus marked, but that knowledge is long forgotten elsewhere in Camlanta."

"It was real," Drom said. "But they need not be who they claimed. I don't credit creatures of faery controlling the fates of humanity."

Cadawn added another branch to the fire. "It need not have been them, but all they said to you is the sort of thing reported by others that have spoken to them. And why should they not appear to you? You have already met their mother."

"Their mother?"

"Of course. The Morrigan is their mother. At least so our lore tells us."

"Some legends claim she is another sister," Ariane said.

"The druids have heard those. The relations of the creatures of faery are not well understood. Our information comes from Conhain though, at least on this point, and he was not one to claim knowledge he did not have."

Drom was not quite satisfied. He did not care much what creatures of faery were related to others.

"What does it mean though? Why speak to me?"

"Ah, it matters greatly," Cadawn said. "And the sisters would not be unaware that I'd form this conclusion. It's proof, of a kind, that this is the moment of prophecy. Now, the future of the realm will be chosen. If we fail, it might be another thousand years, or longer, before the Dark is challenged again. They came to see you, and to judge you. The sisters are neutral. They did not offer help, did they?"

"No."

"And yet they gave it anyway. They confirmed that we are the Guide, Protector and Kindler. Be in no doubt, They would not have come to you in your dreams, and perhaps they will yet come to me and Ariane, even if we don't remember, unless you were an instrument of fate."

It was an answer, of a kind. And if the Thee Sisters came to the Light, they probably went to the Dark as well. So each side knew this was no ordinary battle. Both sides would be informed, and both sides would be desperate.

"One last thing," he said. "They seemed to cast some spell of forgetfulness upon me. Yet I remembered. How is that possible?"

Cadawn stared into the flames. "I wish I knew. That gave me pause for thought. If the Three Sisters cast a spell of forgetfulness, how can you remember? They have great power. I'm not sure even I could withstand such an enchantment. Not in my dreams anyway. And yet *you* did.

Why might turn out to be important. Maybe it was the magic of the sword that interfered with their spell. Or maybe something else. I can't say. Ariane says your mind is strong. Perhaps it was that. Whatever may be, I think you surprised them before they cast their enchantment."

They rode soon after breakfast, and Drom was wary. It seemed creatures of faery haunted every corner of Camlanta, and if they were usually hidden they came out now. He had seen his share, and he wished no more.

The Morrigan he had a liking for. But she was a warrior creature, and he understood her. What purpose did the others have? Or any purpose at all other than to come and look upon a battle as the audience did at the arena, cheering on one side, cursing another, and ready to do it all again the next day and maybe take different sides for the sport of it.

It was a land empty of people. A sense of the wild flowed through it, a sense that out here they could roam for days and see no person at all, not even a traveler from far places by chance crossing their path on the way to somewhere else. Yet there were signs that once it was not so.

They came to an abandoned village. Nothing was left but a few stone hearths, the huts around them long ago rotted or burned, and a thin track that must have served as a main road once, the soil hardened by so much traffic over centuries that even now grass struggled to grow.

"I've been here before," Drom said. "This place is familiar. In my youth we passed through here to put on a show in a far country."

Ariane gazed at him with her large eyes, green and swelling with emotion.

"How old were you when you first started fighting in the arena?"

"Sixteen," he answered. "But I was eighteen on the trip that came through here, an old hand in the arena by then, and already I'd survived more bouts than I care to remember."

They looked at him, and he felt their pity. Perhaps he deserved it, but they did not know that, at least at that stage, he enjoyed it. The crowds cheering his name, even if it was just Isarn early in his career, was more intoxicating than wine. The hard training shaped him and gave him discipline. If he had the strong mind they said he did, it was the training that gave it to him. Then it was honed before the crowds where one mistake was death.

Whatever was bad about him had been brought to the fore by being a gladiator. Whatever was good, likewise, was enhanced. Just as a woodcarver whittled a piece of timber not to a predetermined shape he had in mind but bringing out of the raw material the shape it was disposed to naturally.

"The Broken Lands are ahead," Cadawn said. "I haven't been there, but I know stories of them. They're part of the East March. Just as here, no one dwells there."

"Why are they called broken?" Drom asked. He glanced at Ariane, but she was falling a little behind, a look of concentration on her face.

"They're wild hills," the druid said. "And desolate. Not much grows there save withered grass and stunted trees. It's said that great battles were fought there in the Shadowed Wars, and that vast magics were unleashed that destroyed the land. So it may be. Or perhaps the hills were always like that."

Drom glanced back again. Ariane had stopped, and her head was tilted to the side as if listening.

"What is it?"

She looked at him, her gaze momentarily confused, and then certain.

"Evil comes."

"The gortha is dead," Drom answered.

"Even so, something comes, and it is an abomination born of the Dark."

10. As You Command

The throne room of the palace in Camlanta was Conmah's favorite place. Here he got to play the role he had assigned himself of fool more than anywhere else. It was a role that had kept him alive, but he was tired of it today.

There were few people here. His chamberlain, as always. Insufferable cretin that he was. The vizier, wise fool who could not see what was right in front of his eyes, and a few courtiers, willing to compliment anyone for anything in the hope to curry favor.

He wished them all dead. All the more so because he had been close to death himself. He would never go hunting again. The forest could keep its deer and pheasants and witches of faery. When the time came, he might burn it all to the ground.

He tensed his arm, and reveled in his strength. Once again, the vizier had restored him to youth with the rites. Yet he was not as young as he had been. The magic was less potent now, something that he had been noticing for a while. Or else Arofel had withheld something from him.

It was time to work on her again. She had revealed here and there some of the magic words of the rites, and promised him more. When he knew all, then he could reveal himself as a true king. The vizier would no longer be needed, and the goddess would have a better vessel for her earthly power. The vizier, for all his lore and magic lacked true ambition. Camlanta was enough for him. But the world beckoned, and Arofel could have it through a king who was not afraid of war.

The oak doors to the throne room opened, and a guard announced a visitor.

"Your Majesty, the bard Tassalind requests audience."

Conmah giggled and clapped. "Good! Send him in. All this talk of taxes and guilds and street repair that we have been having is just so awfully dull."

The guard bowed, but gave no answer. Conmah could sense his repugnance and clapped even harder. They hated him, but that same man who abhorred him now would be quick to beg a favor tomorrow. They were all hypocrites.

Tassalind entered. He looked vaguely scruffy as always, and his cloak, crimson with gold hems, was stained by travel and food. He did a little jump, rolled to the ground and came up in a bow.

Conmah clapped, and the bard smiled broadly. That smile did not reach his eyes though. They were hard, and Conmah knew they had noted everyone in the room, where they were standing and how they were armed. And if his gaze lingered even less on the vizier, there was reason for that.

"Sire," the bard said. "May I entertain you. I have acquired some new tricks."

"Really? That's wonderful! Tell me, have you mastered the fourth knife yet when juggling?"

The bard gave a shrug. "Perhaps. Perhaps not, sire. Command me, and you will see."

The vizier chose that moment to interrupt. "With your leave I shall go, Your Majesty. I have much work to do."

"So soon, Castanuin? Never mind. You know what you're doing. Sometimes I think it's really you who runs the kingdom. You have so many responsibilities."

The druid looked at him without humor. They both knew the vizier was in charge and made all decisions, but the vizier did not wish it to seem so.

67

"Your Majesty is far too kind." The words were uttered in a tone that suggested he was speaking to a simpleton, and reeked of condescension. Conmah pretend not to notice and waved at him like a little girl saying goodbye to a playmate.

As the vizier strode out of the room Conmah pointed to the courtiers.

"Best if you leave as well for half an hour. I want to watch the bard perform. It's the king's prerogative to see that first. Isn't it?"

"Yes, sire," one of them answered. They did not wish to leave. No doubt some at least had favors to ask, but they knew they would have their chance afterward. Especially if the vizier remained busy elsewhere.

The bard grinned, then did a backward somersault landing on his feet.

"Hooray!" the king cried. "Splendid! Do it again!"

There was only the two of them left in the throne room now, save for the chamberlain.

Tassalind jumped and rolled and came up into a high leap. Suddenly there were two knives in his hand, though Conmah had not even seen them being drawn. They spun in loops in the air as he juggled them, and then he began to walk in a circle.

"More! More!" cried the king.

The bard kept going as he was, but suddenly out of nowhere a third knife had appeared. His hands moved faster now, and the knives were thrown a little higher. He made it look easy.

"Another!" the king said, clapping. "Another!"

"As you command."

The bard stopped walking the circle. Now he stood on one leg, then raised himself on tiptoes. Conmah wondered at the strength of his foot and his balance, and when he looked upward again four blades were spinning in the air.

"You've done it. Marvelous! You're the best in the world!"

"Perhaps I am," the bard replied, answering even as he went on. Then he caught the knives one by one, sheathing them in turn until the last had disappeared.

The king clapped. "A gold coin to him," he instructed the chamberlain.

Without comment the chamberlain did as instructed, and the bard received the coin, flicked it in the air with one hand and snatched it in the other.

The chamberlain shuffled back, unimpressed by anything, to his usual spot a little behind the king.

"Be a good fellow," Conmah said to him, "and check with the cook on preparations for tonight's party. I hear he has a wonderful new recipe for grilled duck. I just can't wait."

"I'm sure it will be duck and it will be grilled, sire."

"Oh dear. You have no appreciation for the finer details. Please go talk to him and tell me exactly what he says."

The chamberlain eyed the bard, and Conmah hid his annoyance.

"Never mind him," the king said. "I'm perfectly safe. He's only a bard after all, and the guards are at the door."

"As you wish, sire."

The chamberlain shambled away to a side door near the back of the room. If he were capable of moving fast, Conmah had never seen it. He was surrounded by idiots, the incompetent and the lazy.

Not the bard though. He now had a pipe in his hand and had begun to play a delightful tune, skipping and hopping as he did so.

The door shut behind them, and the bard continued a few moments then he put away the pipe and straightened to his full height. Had the others seen him now, a fierce expression on his face and all pretense at entertaining shed like a cloak, they would have been surprised.

"Your chamberlain mistrusts me," the bard said.

"If he knew who you were, I think I'd see him move fast for the first time in his life."

The dark eyes of the bard glanced away from the closed door and fell on the king.

"He would not get far no matter how fast he ran."

That was certainly true. In this man the king had found a kindred spirit, and an ally. He too played the fool. Yet he was swift of mind and practiced of skill. The others did not realize that his ability to juggle knives could be put to use to throw them. Nor that when he wielded the slender blade at his side he could kill any swordsman in the palace. By repute, he could slay with a dozen poisons too, or use a dozen more to invoke madness, tractability or delirium. For he was an assassin, and he hid his true self as well as Conmah hid his own.

"We don't have long alone," Conmah said. "Have you studied the vizier?"

"I have. I know his habits, and the paths he walks, especially between here and his own palace. I can kill him at any time. Shall I?"

Conmah thought hard. The time was not yet ripe, no matter how much he wished it. He had not yet fully learned the rites that kept him young, and until then he could not act. Nor was he so sure of the assassin. He knew he was good. His skill was dazzling. Yet against magic, what defense could he muster. Even so, a dead druid cast no magic. Surprise countered all.

Then there were the other druids. He must give more thought about them. Should the archdruid die, another would rise in his place. He could not kill them all, so he must find a pretext to send his soldiers against them. After all, no matter how strong they were, they could not defeat an army.

"Not yet," he said with regret. "Stay ready. I don't think it will be long. Perhaps another few months."

"As you wish."

Conmah slipped him a bag of gold coins. The assassin would be in no hurry. The longer this went on the more money he made, but with that came the risk of discovery. Still, neither could possibly be suspected.

"You should know," the bard said, "the archdruid is worried lately. You know better than I what events are occurring in the realm, and how long they'll last, but while he's preoccupied like that, he'll be easier to catch off guard."

Conmah shook his head. "Wait. I think he may be preoccupied for a while yet. If that changes, I'll let you know. Suffice to say that there *is* a threat to him, and a great one. Nor do his underlings have it under control. I'll know if and when they do, but I think we have at least a few weeks. And there are things I need to … learn as well. Anyway, it will give you time to study him more."

"As you command, my king."

It was quiet in the throne room, and the bard was standing close. Conmah did not doubt there were secret spy holes, though he had never discovered them. If someone were listening though, they could not have heard anything. Even so, the longer such a personal conversation went on the more suspicious it would look should anyone be watching.

Conmah gestured slightly at the walls. "Continue, bard. I would see more of your splendid tricks."

Tassalind understood at once what was required. He bowed, then did a backward somersault and began to juggle once more. It was the knives again, and to the king's

71

shock he saw there were now five blades spinning in the air.

It had taken him years to find such a man, for all negotiations must be deadly secret. Yet he had found him at last, and hope surged within him. Soon, he would be rid of the druids. He would be king in his own right. And immortal. Then he would lead armies to conquest in the name of Arofel.

11. The Warrior-spell

Cadawn took thought. The little group had no definite leader, but the archdruid was the one most suited to the role. He had knowledge greater than theirs of many things, and generally Drom and Ariane deferred to him.

"I cannot sense any evil," he said. "Your powers are different from mine, Ariane, and I think you're more attuned to malevolence. You detect that whereas I'm more likely to sense a displacement of the natural order of the wilderness around us."

Drom did not much care. He trusted both of them when they said such things, and his hand gripped his sword hilt.

Cadawn noticed it. "We may have to fight in the end," he said, "but for now let's ride and see if we can put distance between us and whatever it is. Who knows? It might not even be connected to us at all. This is a wild land, and there's evil in the world apart from anything the Court Druids may send against us."

Ariane did not reply, but Drom could tell by her expression that she did not think it any coincidence. Something was coming for them, and if the gortha was dead it was something else.

They mounted and rode. Cadawn led, and the other two followed side by side. It was not a fast gallop. That would achieve nothing except to tire the horses. It was not slow though, and the green grass flowed smoothly under them and the hills in the distance they soon climbed and saw new ones ahead that were climbed in turn.

Drom looked back from time to time. He saw nothing. Ariane, if anything, looked more concerned and he knew now, beyond doubt, they were pursued.

The hills were not steep. The grass was becoming short and dry though, and ahead were a cluster of hills, taller than the ones they had crested so far, and seemingly barren. They looked to be mostly dirt and rock, and there were no trees and not even much grass.

It was an eerie place, and unlike anything Drom had seen before. It was quiet, and there were few birds and no animals. No doubt there were more than could be seen, for the three strangers rode into the land with noise. Whatever was here would long since have seen or heard them and hidden.

Drom studied the landscape. What magic or sorcery could do such a thing? Mile after mile seemed blasted, and there were signs that even some of the rocks had melted. He could not be sure though because wind and water had eroded much.

Most of all, he feared there was no cover here in which to find a place to hide both riders and mounts.

They slowed as the hills grew steeper. The only cover was to ride in the valleys between them, but they found the earth in those places dusty and dangerous. Hollows that could break the leg of a horse were filled with soft dirt or dead grasses or stinking mud that dried on the surface and was hard to see but underneath was a death trap.

In the end, they resorted to the hilltops again, going from crest to crest where they were more visible but safe from the hazards below.

From the crest of one such hill they saw a party of riders emerge on their backtrail. They were closer than Drom would have believed, but no doubt they had seen their quarry first and taken good steps to conceal themselves.

"Who is it?" Cadawn asked.

"It must be the druid," Drom answered. "Though how he found us so soon I don't know."

Ariane shaded her eyes with a hand and was silent a moment.

"The druid, yes. But he has invoked a magic that I haven't felt before, or one was invoked upon him."

Cadawn brushed a fly away from his face, and the ears of his mount flicked.

"I feel it now, too," he said. "It's strange, whatever it is."

A mosquito landed on Drom's hand, and he brushed it away. The land was desolate, yet still it seemed to breed all manner of pests. He would be happy to leave it behind, and swiftly.

"Our horses are still strong. I say we gallop, and see if the enemy can keep up."

"I'm not sure," Cadawn answered. "There are more of them than us, but if they've found us once they'll find us again. Better to fight them now than always be looking over our shoulders, especially when we camp at night."

It was a good point. The pursuers were close enough that they could catch up if they rode after dark. Drom did not wish to wake to the sensation of steel against his throat.

"Then we ride for now," he said. "And keep an eye open for a good defensive position. If we find one, we'll rest and prepare."

They moved ahead at a good pace, not bothering to try to conceal themselves. The enemy already knew where they were, and even if they didn't this was the worst possible place to try to hide their trail.

Afternoon cast a golden light over the land, and made it seem more beautiful that it was. Ahead lay a dark pool of shadows in a deeper vale than most, and Drom studied it hard.

"Those aren't shadows," he said at length. "I think they're trees. The first we've seen in this desolate place."

Cadawn drew his mount to a halt and looked as well, almost eagerly.

"I wonder," he said as if to himself.

There was no more time for talk. The enemy were close, and they all knew instinctively that a forest, even a small one, offered opportunity for concealment and defense. If nothing else, it would stop a charge by a larger force of riders.

Cadawn led the way down. It even seemed as though there were a path, so ancient that most traces of it had been washed away by dirt and sand. Yet in places, protected by the slope against rain and the detritus within running water, a flat surface of stone remained, with a camber in the center and a gutter to each side. So it appeared to Drom, anyway.

It was a long way down. The slope was not steep, but it kept going, and often the path, or road if such it was, looped around less certain ground. Cadawn, coming from the swamp as he did, followed the track meticulously.

Drom did not expect quagmires here, but the druid might be right to be cautious. It slowed them down, but the ancients did nothing by accident, and if they went around something there was good reason. Probably the terrain was steep, or under water in wet weather.

At length they drew close to the bottom of the valley. Drom looked back, but there was no sign of the riders. They would be close though. It would not be long before the sound of battle echoed around the rocky slopes of this silent valley.

The trees were pines. They were not of a sort that Drom knew, and he supposed that whatever they were they were especially adapted to the harsh climate here, and had somehow escaped the blasting magics that had seared the rest of the land.

Perhaps being a deeper valley than most had spared this place. There were even swards of grass here, though much of the soil was still barren.

Cadawn stopped, and Drom and Ariane came up beside him. From now on they could ride abreast.

"I've heard stories of this place," the druid said. "I had thought it miles to our east, but obviously not."

"What stories?" Drom asked. The forest did not look evil to him, but it was eerie and dark.

"Just rumors of a forest amid the desolation. It might be that more than one such place exists here."

"Rumors of magic," Ariane said. "I can sense a strange power over the land, brooding."

The druid nudged his horse forward. "Yes. Magic. But magic of faery rather than of the druids. It's strong here. The land wears it like a man might a cloak."

They went ahead, and soon the dark eaves of the forest reached out and overshadowed them. Even so, the path was easy to follow. Here, the forces of time had been kept at bay, and they followed a road beyond all doubt.

It was not just a road. Drom, judging from the sun before they entered, decided it ran due east. He could not be sure of that, but the rising sun was important in the legends of Camlanta, and doubly so for the creatures of faery. The other two sensed magic, but he detected it too via the books he had read in his youth.

The archdruid had paid little attention to him when he visited and read books of lore. Or borrowed them. It was amusing to him, but Drom had quietly amassed a wealth of knowledge that would shame many scholars in the capital cities. He knew it, and it was not just knowledge for the sake of it. It had saved his life more than once, and might do so again.

Later, he had acquired wealth too. That was stashed in secret locations across the realm, and in private accounts that not even the vizier could track.

Knowledge was power. Ignorance death. Wealth a means to an end. He brought his mind back to the present as he rode though. He did not trust this forest, for where there was magic there was also power.

The trees cast groping shadows. The trunks were arrow straight, and the forest floor covered in the detritus of eons of leaf fall. It was silent, and even the trotting of the horses' hooves on the hard road made little noise. Then something occurred to him.

"This is a road," he said to Cadawn. "In its day it must have been a grand avenue. It must lead somewhere important. Do the rumors you've heard say what?"

The druid raised his eyebrows. "Your wit is as sharp as your sword. If this is the place I think it is, then we'll find a ring of standing stones at the end of the road. There the magic of this vale will be strongest, and though the creatures of faery rarely show themselves, and still less interfere in the events important to humanity, the power of that place will help me, for I am a druid."

"As is your opponent," Drom said.

"Yes, but he has chosen a different path from the druids of old. His strength and power are now hitched to the goddess Arofel. Mine is more in tune with faery. With the powers of nature."

The trees grew taller as they went ahead, and the shadows darker. Then they came to an area where the forest thinned, and swiftly to an open glade. Just as Cadawn had hoped, a ring of standing stones stood there.

Time had worn the stones. Snow and ice and heat and driving rain had smitten them for eons. Lichen and moss grew on them. Yet still they were a sight of awe. The ring was vast, and the single stones that made it were the largest Drom had ever seen. It would have taken a hundred men to move one a foot. If they could move such massive objects at all. But there were thirteen of them, sunk in the ground and as firmly in place as they had been set in a time before Camlanta even existed.

"The stories are true," Cadawn said breathlessly.

Drom was vastly impressed, but his mind turned immediately to practical matters of defense.

"It's a much better place to defend than out in the open. I suggest we hold the center, and see what they do. They can't charge us on horseback. They must come in on foot through the gaps in the stones."

They tethered their horses and built a small fire, and kept a supply of fuel nearby for the night. Should the battle not be over and done by then, one way or the other, it would not be safe to venture outside the ring in the dark. The fire, likewise, would light the ring so that no one could creep inside it unseen.

It was pointless trying to hide. The smoke from the fire or its light might give away their location, but the riders coming for them would know it anyway.

The afternoon wore on. They kept a watch in brisk turns while the others snatched a little sleep. It might turn out to be a long night. Drom fell instantly into a deep slumber, and the others envied him. They could not, but he had long ago learned the knack of resting when possible in the arena. The trick was to think of anything but the upcoming fight.

Sunset seemed early in the deep valley. The long shadows of the trees swamped everything out first, and then a mist, silver white, rose from the ground and flowed like rivers down the aisles of the trees.

Night fell, and there were noises from outside. Drom could hear no voices, but he was sure once he heard the jingle of harness and a blade drawn from its sheath.

"They're out there," Cadawn said.

Ariane stared into the silvery gloom. "Why don't they attack?"

"The druid is there. I sense his magic. And his uncertainty. He fears the powers of faery, and of old such rings as this were sacred. They were places of rites. The midwinter and midsummer solstice in particular. The creatures of faery would gather and feast at those times, and men acquired those rituals too. It was a time of peace, of setting aside feuds and where chiefs settled grievances among their peoples, and between neighboring peoples. Strife was forbidden. He senses all that, and he wonders if there is any power of faery still here to enforce harmony."

"Is there?" Drom asked.

"There is great power here still, but I think faery will remain neutral. If we are to survive this, it will be by our own skill."

Drom shrugged. "That goes both ways. If the enemy attacks, they must prevail by their own strength alone."

There was something else at play too. He knew druids, and for all their great magic they were as scared of dying as anyone else. The druid out there knew that his soldiers would fall swiftly at Drom's hands, and that Cadawn possessed a magic likely greater than his own. He was in no rush to attack, despite his greater numbers. So too, the night time dark was their enemy. It sowed confusion, and it would be hard to tell friend from foe.

It was a long night. They heard whispers from time to time, and the neighs of horses. There was movement in the mists too, and it was all around them. Here and there was a gleam of naked blades, or an arm raised or a stealthy footstep, not quite stealthy enough.

Dawn finally came, and still there was no attack. With the increasing light came a breeze, and the mists rolled away into the forest and revealed what was hidden through the night.

The druid was there, and his soldiers. Cadawn studied them for a little while, and whispered.

"This will be worse than I thought."

12. The Fury of the Dark

Drom eyed the enemy closely. They were on foot, and they shuffled and twitched. Swords were drawn, sheathed, and drawn again. For those who were closest, there was a red and haggard look to their eyes.

"The warrior-spell is upon them," he said. His own sword was in his hands, but he held it casually.

Cadawn glanced at him keenly. "You know much about things few people even guess at."

"That may be. But I've had the ill-fortune to have been hunted for much of my life, including by soldiers treated as these. The end is not good for them, whether we manage to kill them or not."

The sun rose higher, and the enemy came into better sight. Behind them was the druid, but of him they could only catch glimpses between the fidgeting soldiers.

"How shall we beat them then?"

Drom did not hesitate. "The best way is to delay them. They're working themselves into a fury now, fueled by the magic of the druid. They'll be faster, stronger, and unafraid of injury or death. Only killing them will stop them. Wounding, even badly, will not hinder their assault when it finally comes. Everything has a price though. They cannot maintain that intensity. It burns out their body and minds. If we fled, we might stay ahead of them for a few hours. Long enough for them to weaken."

One of the soldiers picked up a stone and flung it at them. It missed. Cadawn barely seemed to notice, for he was deep in thought.

"The same spell would then be placed on the horses. I don't think we would get far. We would have to fight anyway, but not in a place of our choosing."

Straightening, the druid looked suddenly decisive. He had made up his mind about something.

"You're correct. Half a day, or a bit longer, is as much as they can last. And we must do something soon, for they're near to being ready to charge."

One of them came close to the ring, and he stared at them with hatred gleaming in his wide eyes. It was more than hatred though. Insanity was in that expression as well. Drom knew the look, and he hated the Court Druids for it. Killing a man was one thing, but stealing his mind from him was another.

At that moment, the enemy druid came closer, and they could see him for the first time. He looked haggard as did the soldiers, and his eyes were red and raw. Malice shone in them, and there was an air about him of magic though as yet he made no threat.

"He is the source of the evil," Ariane whispered. "He reeks of it."

Drom was not sure what she meant. All the Court Druids were evil in their way, or worshipped it. This one might be worse, or she might mean something else. Certainly there was something unwholesome to his look, but it was more like something had been done to him than something arising from his own nature.

"Speak your name," Cadawn commanded. "And ask your terms."

Drom understood at once that this was merely an attempt at delay. The enemy druid should know that, but it still had to be tried.

The hands of the druid gripped tight, and his eyes strained at them.

83

"You need not know my name. And my terms are simple. You are required to die."

His voice was harsh, and he spoke like a person who was recovering from a long illness. Something was indeed wrong with him, but Drom could not decide what.

Cadawn laughed. "I think you have things the wrong way around. It is you, Amrog, who will die. Yes, I know your name. I know all the rebel ragtag that cavorts around Camalduin, pretending to practice magic but instead worshipping Arofel. Why don't you join the true druids instead? I can teach you magics to astound you."

The Court Druid looked at him blankly. Something was seriously wrong with him, and even his mind seemed scattered as though unable to concentrate on a simple conversation.

"There is only one true magic, and one true power in the world. To her you will submit. In death."

"Come show us then. Come and attack. Come and die." Suddenly Cadawn was different. He was not the easy-going travel companion that he had been. He looked as he had when he slew the gortha, and there was a majesty about him greater than any king and a surety in his posture of victory.

Cadawn stuck out a long arm and pointed at the soldiers. He spoke to them now and ignored Amrog.

"Men of Camlanta, look into your hearts. You are bewitched. The warrior-spell is upon you, driving you, pushing you on, burning you from within like a fire. Can you not feel it? It will consume you. It can be resisted though. You might live. Walk away. Renounce battle and war and seek peace. I beseech you, abandon the fool who leads you into death. He cares nothing for you, and will not remember even your names when you are gone."

The soldiers stirred at that. Most seemed to grow even more agitated though. They were too far gone, but one came closer and glanced at Cadawn before stepping out of view again. Drom had seen him however. It was the farmer Catagern, and he was a long way from home and further out of his depth.

He should have fled when Drom spared his life, but maybe the druid had put an even stronger fear upon him.

Amrog shuddered as though he were in a fever, and then he stilled. Some of the redness left his eyes, and when he spoke his voice was less harsh.

"Surrender. All three of you, surrender. If you do, I promise to take you to the capital where you'll receive a fair trial, and maybe even the mercy of the king and archdruid. Otherwise, you will die a horrible death. Look at my men. You know it to be true."

The soldiers had worked themselves to a higher state of fury while their leader spoke. Drom could sense they were ready to attack now, and even Amrog would soon lose control of them. Cadawn had attempted delay, but it was not long enough. Hours were needed rather than minutes.

To his surprise, Ariane spoke next. Her voice was as music compared to Amrog's, and there was a power of conviction in what she said that surely even the enemy must fear.

"We do not surrender. We will never surrender, for the Light of Aroth is upon us, and no Dark can extinguish it. You do not know your peril. Go now in peace. Look into your hearts and find the Light there, for it is in each of us. Prepare for the coming of Aroth, for even as the sun rises he will return."

Amrog, trembling, went white and then red. Some battle was going on in his mind, and then he laughed. Drom knew before he spoke that whatever ailed him had conquered. There was a sorcery upon him, likely cast by the archdruid. Who else could do so?

The sorcery had leeched into his soul. Twisted already, it had found fertile ground in which to grow. Drom had not seen its like before, but he feared it. It was like the warrior-spell, but cast upon a druid of great power. There was no way to know what would happen next, but it was going to be terrible.

Amrog seemed to swell. Power was about him like a cloak now, and even Cadawn took a step back. The soldiers began to creep forward, and then their leader screamed out.

"Kill them! Kill them all! Tear them apart!"

The soldiers rushed forward. Yet Cadawn was quicker than they. He brought his arms together above his head, and the hathlinden clasped about his forearms clashed together. There was a peal like a giant bell, beautiful but ominous, and with it a flash of silvery light that blinded.

Drom shielded his eyes and held high his sword. The blade of it thrummed, and then the light flew from standing stone to standing stone until all thirteen of them flared silver bright.

Cadawn lowered his arms, but the magic of the standing stones spun round them now in a circle.

The enemy outside could not be seen, though one at least of them tried to break through. There was a scream, and a column of dark smoke rose up in the air. After that, it was silent.

Ariane went to the druid. He was pale, and seemed shaky on his feet.

"Are you well?"

"I will be in a few moments. It was no great magic, but I'm not yet fully recovered from the gortha."

"It seems a great magic to me," Drom said.

"It is. But not mine. This is a place of enormous natural power. For that reason the ring of stones was built here,

86

and the stones have their own … essence. All I did was bring it forth."

The druid was recovering swiftly, and the color was coming back to him.

"How long will it last?" Ariane asked.

Cadawn looked around him. "I'm not sure. I was not even sure I could do it. The rings are meant for another purpose, but that knowledge is lost to the druids. The light should go on for few hours, I think."

It would not be long enough, Drom knew. He had seen the warrior-spell at work before, and the soldiers would still be alive. They would be weakened though. The fury of battle would still be on them, for the magic drove them regardless. Yet their bodies would burn from within. That was the way it had looked to him, and he wished that on no man, not even his enemies.

They rested within the ring. At times there was a cry from without, and once the clang of blades followed by a booming command from Amrog.

"They fight among themselves," Ariane said.

"The magic consumes them," Cadawn answered. "It exhorts them to battle, and if they cannot be soon directed at their chosen target, they might fall upon each other."

"Or upon Amrog," Drom said.

"He is in danger too. It'll help him though that he has commanded them for some time now. Had he cast the spell over strangers, then the more easily would they turn on him."

It was well past mid-morning before the first signs showed that the magic was running its course. The silver light was not as bright, and the enemy beyond was clearer.

Amrog tried to speed up the process. At times there was a flash like lightning, followed by a boom. Yet it seemed not to change the spinning magic of the stones in the least.

87

"Tire yourself out, Amrog. Fool that you are," Cadawn muttered.

Drom was not so sure it was foolish. Trying to break through might be the only way to keep the soldiers focused on their true target rather than turning on themselves.

The magic began to falter. It had lasted until nearly noon, and though that was not long enough the soldiers outside would have spent much of their energy in fruitless seething. They were like a stick of wood in the fireplace. They had burned, and much was gone, yet what was left could still flare to life if moved. They were about to flare now, and they still greatly outnumbered the three defenders within the standing stones.

Drom drew his sword, and it felt good in his hand. He was rested, but now the thought of battle roused his blood, and he breathed deep.

Standing straight and tall, Cadawn prepared himself mentally. He could kill many soldiers, but he would know that he must reserve himself instead to combat Amrog. Magic must defend against magic.

Ariane seemed tense, but there was a light in her green eyes that burned with determination. Drom was not sure of her powers, but she was unafraid, and he had seen her defend herself before. The enemy might be surprised by her, and so might he be.

The magic faltered and ran out. Gone was the silver light, and all that was left was the yellow light of daytime. In the distance the pine trees were dark. Bulking up before that view were the soldiers, swords drawn, haggard faces staring, and behind them Amrog, his own face contorted.

Drom saw the farmer. He was in the middle of the soldiers, and he had a sword now. Red rimmed his eyes, and hatred was in them. Even so, he had resisted the warrior-spell better than the others. He did not look crazed, but merely angry. Even a little scared.

"Go home and tend your farm, Catagern. Live!"

The farmer did not answer, but at that same moment Amrog screamed.

"Charge! Kill them all!"

13. An Army if Need Be

The soldiers rushed in. They did not converge from all directions, but tumbled through the gap in the ring of stones nearest Amrog like a river hurtling between its banks.

Drom knew it was his task to stem the tide. He strode forward to meet them, and the first fell to a slashing cut that was too swift for an ordinary soldier's defenses. His head fell to the left and his body to the right.

Cadawn would only intervene when he must. His main task was the other druid. Ariane could protect herself, yet still Drom positioned himself ahead of her.

A soldier leaped over the dead body, screaming wildly, his face contorted and eyes lost in a miasma of fury. Drom did not kill him. Instead he shoulder charged him and sent him flying backward into the following soldiers. They stumbled and fell, or swerved to avoid him.

Drom was among them then, his blade a blur of steel. Three men he slew before the others even recovered from the obstacle he had put in their path. The man he had shouldered rose to his feet, and died for it to make four.

The others, crazed as they were, paid scant heed. Battle lust was upon them, but even so they hesitated a moment.

Their pause, if only for a heartbeat, gave Drom time to seize the initiative again. He performed a move known in the arena as the escaping fish. Leaping to their left, he landed nimbly, then leaped to the right and forward so he was unexpectedly in their midst again.

The zigzag movement was dangerous. If they reacted quickly he could meet several sword thrusts. Yet for all their battle frenzy, they were not great swordsmen.

He was among them once more, hacking, slashing and stabbing.

Steel rang against steel this time. Some blocked his strokes, and some jumped back. Either way, they died. But the others, outnumbering him and not afraid of death as they should be, clambered over their fallen comrades to come at him, howling and screaming like animals as they did.

From the corner of his eye he saw that Ariane had retrieved a sword from a fallen soldier and set upon them from the other side. She was skilled with the blade, which she held in her right hand. Her left was raised as well, a white light glowing upon her palm.

Drom yelled a battle cry, and thrust himself right into the heart of his opponents. Often the last thing an enemy expected was the thing that killed them.

A sword arced toward his head, and he ducked. Even at that moment a knife was thrust at him. It was close quarter fighting now, and hard to find room to swing a blade. The knife took him with a glancing blow, and he kicked one man in the groin, smashed another with the pommel of his sword, and spun around with a little more room until his blade decapitated another man. Then he was beside Ariane.

She had killed a man herself, and they shunned the light from her palm. The Cult of Aroth was all for peace and tranquility, yet someone had taught her to fight for herself, and passed on skill with a blade. To whoever that was, his gratitude went out to them.

The remaining soldiers were still wrapped in a mindless fury. Normal men would have retreated by now, either to regroup or to flee depending on the quality of their leadership. These were different. They screamed as animals and charged again.

Drom stood before Ariane, and in that moment he was back in the arena. His confidence was supreme, and the crowd chanted his name. He stood poised and relaxed, ready to unleash hell on earth.

They did not reach him. Cadawn thrust his fingers forth in a stabbing motion, and fire darted. It rolled into the soldiers, twined among them, wrapped itself around limbs and torsos, and burned.

The men screamed. Yet even dying they came for Drom. One he slew with a deft cut to the neck, opening an artery. The other lost a hand, and when he grabbed at Drom's neck with the other, Drom's blade severed that too, and then flicked back to stab the man in the head. He fell, but crawled toward Drom, driven by sorcery.

A final thrust killed him, and Drom leaped back into a guard position, ready for more attacks.

The soldiers were finally beaten though. The few who remained burned and screamed, falling to the ground. The stench of blackened flesh and death filled the air, and the magnificent ring of stones had become a ghastly place of slaughter.

Cadawn stood where he had, smoke rising between him and the Court Druid. Amrog stepped forward. He looked at his fallen men contemptuously.

"They have served their purpose," he said. "And you are weakened now. Many of my order have dreamed of this moment. To have you, the rebel leader, in their power. A thousand years it has taken but it comes to me at last."

The smoke cleared, and Cadawn stood just as he had. The hathlinden gleamed on his forearms, and something of their light was in his eyes.

"A thousand years it has taken? Had any of your kind the courage you could have entered Car Sagoth and challenged our leader to combat. You have not, for you fear us. Our power is older, and truer, more fitting to humanity. And while you lick the feet of Arofel, we have studied and learned from northern shamans and eastern wizards. We are strong. Your days of rule draw to a close, and your own life is over. I know not what sorcery is cast upon you, but your master has discarded you like a broken tool. He will take up another when you are gone, and think no more of you than an ant crushed beneath his boot."

The other man laughed. "Take up another tool? I do not think so. Never. It is you and your kind that will perish."

As he spoke Amrog made a whipping motion with his arms, and a sudden wind hurtled at them. Drom bent down against it, shielding his eyes from a spray of debris. Small pebbles smashed into him, and twigs and leaves cut at his skin.

Against the magic Cadawn lifted both arms, and spread his palms outward in a sign of negation. The wind ceased.

"I don't wish to kill you," he said. "Return to your master. Or denounce him."

"Never!"

If Amrog had been impressed by the ease with which his sorcery was defeated, he did not show it. His cry had been one of fervor rather than irritation.

He moved again, this time slowly. His arms lifted in the air, palm upward.

Drom wondered why Cadawn did not kill him. Perhaps there was some etiquette to druidic duels that he did not understand. Or, more likely, it was a sign of Cadawn's character. Evil as the Court Druids were, they remained his brothers in ancient lore. Once they had been a single order.

The ground heaved. Drom fell and rolled, and he came up sword before him. Ariane was beside him, coming to her feet also.

Strangely, the great ring of stones did not seem to move. They were rooted to the ground not by weight, but by magic.

Cadawn gave a sudden twist of his wrist. The movement of the earth ceased, except for a single crack that ran directly at Amrog. The druid leaped to the side, but he was never in danger. The crack was deep, yet not wide. Drom thought it was kept that way deliberately.

With a clap of his hands Cadawn closed the narrow chasm.

"You are no match for me, brother. Especially in this place where the old powers are strong. The powers of faery that you have abandoned."

It seemed to grow cold within the ancient ring. Despite the daylight, it grew dark also. It was like twilight, and the shadow of the thirteen stones stretched forth like creeping things, alive and with intent.

"See!" Cadawn proclaimed. "The old forces are waking. They have no love for humanity, but less for those that serve other powers."

Amrog seethed where he stood, and his haggard face looked more like his soldiers' every moment. Whatever sorcery he had invoked, or had been laid upon him, ate away at his soul like the warrior-spell, only for a druid it must be worse. A druid had great power of mind and body, and they were conduits for magic. Drom felt a chill run through him. However this ended, it would not be well.

The Court Druid opened his mouth, but no words came. His eyes were wild, and he stabbed his hands forward. Crimson fire sizzled from them, and rolled forward as a wall.

Drom stood before Ariane, shielding her. Yet Cadawn was quicker. He raised his hands and uttered a word of power that cracked the air like a whip.

Amrog was flung backward, and the sorcerous flame went out like a campfire on which a bucket of water had been thrown. Yet he came to his feet instantly. He was not done nor beaten.

He stood in the shadow of a standing stone, and he began to chant. Cadawn could have stopped him. It was clear now who possessed the greater power, but instead he merely spoke.

"Cease, brother! We can talk. Something ails you, though I don't know what. Together we can seek a cure."

Amrog paused. For what purpose, Drom did not know. Even as he watched though, a second figure emerged from behind the standing stone. It was Catagern the farmer, and Drom felt relief that he had not died. The warrior-spell was upon him, but he had resisted it.

Even so, there was fury in his eyes. It was more that of one who had been wronged than one driven by sorcery, yet it was violent.

With a sudden lunge, the farmer sprang forward. His sword thrust out, and it took Amrog in the lower back. It was not a killing stroke. Not instantly, yet death was still certain.

The druid screamed and fell. Catagern was not done. He hacked again, landing several blows, and one severed a neck artery. Red blood spurted, and then the farmer stood back.

Catagern dropped the bloodied sword. The druid died, and the farmer watched him, horror filling his eyes.

"Do with me as you will," he said into the silence. "Maybe I have committed murder. Or maybe not. I know though that some spell was cast upon me."

95

Drom did not like the man. Not in the least. Even so, his heart went out to him. He had resisted the warrior-spell, yet was not untouched by it. Cold-blooded killing was not his way, but many would say the druid had reaped even as he had sown.

The farmer went to his knees and wept beside the corpse of the druid. He was a ruined man, and his mind could not come to grips with what he had done. Drom understood better though. The spell had not fully captured him, but it had worked on him enough to unseat his normal moral code. It was unfortunate for the druid, for the frenzy that drove the farmer, not as severe as it had been with the soldiers, could be guided by reason. The farmer knew who had cast a spell upon him, and took his revenge.

For Catagern, Drom had a wealth of sympathy. For the druid, none.

Ariane went to the farmer. Drom nearly tried to stop her. He did not entirely trust Catagern, for he was still under the influence of the spell even if he had dropped his weapon. Yet with a glance, Cadawn signaled for him not to intervene.

The farmer looked up at Ariane. "What have I done?"

"You have killed a man," she answered. "There is no hiding that, nor, if I judge you rightly, would you want to. Even so, a great evil has been done to you. You may have heard of the warrior-spell in stories?"

The man nodded, and Ariane continued. "The druid cast it on you and the soldiers. He drove you with a frenzy to kill us. So listen to me carefully. It was your hand that slew, but the mind that directed your frenzy was his. And that spell is still on you, and it might kill you yet."

"I understand."

"Do you repent of your act?"

"I do."

"Then I shall heal you."

Even as she spoke she placed a hand upon his shoulder and a soft white light flowed from it. The features of the farmer eased as though he were about to fall asleep, but he did not. The redness left his eyes, and the gauntness of his face diminished. After a moment, a black shadow fell away from him and his eyes widened.

The farmer stood slowly, and bowed to her.

"Go in peace," she said. "You are cleansed of all evil."

Catagern slowly made to walk away, seemingly dazed or like a man just woken from sleep. Then he turned and spoke to Drom.

"I misjudged you long ago. I'm sorry for that. The stories of you are true, at least the good ones. Know this though." He glanced at Ariane as well. "From what I heard traveling with the druid, they hate you both with a fiery passion. And fear you. This druid might now be dead, but others will come. The vizier will send an army against you if need be."

14. The Trap Is Set

Despite it being noontime, the room was dark. All doors were closed, and the windows heavily draped. Every servant had been warned to stay away.

Castanuin sat in a deep chair, his breathing slow and his mind stilled. He was not awake, nor yet properly asleep. He was in that state between where the druids meditated.

And sometimes worked magic.

He did so now. Since his last meeting with Amrog, the sorcery he had cast connected them both. It did far more, but he was not concerned with that presently.

It was not perfect, but he could see what Amrog saw, and hear what he heard. To some extent, he could perceive the man's thoughts too.

Amrog was deeply troubled. As he should be. He had failed yet again, for he stood without the ring of standing stones and he had not anticipated the rebel druid would draw on their power to block entrance to the circle.

The soldiers were fading. Mortal flesh could not long endure the warrior-spell. However, the tracker was fighting it. He kept aloof from the others, and though controlled by the spell it might break at any moment. All the quicker for Amrog gave him no heed and bent his will instead on the soldiers to prevent them fighting one another.

As a tactic, the warrior-spell had advantages. Amrog had employed it too soon though. He was paying the price for that now, and the man knew it. Castanuin could feel his chagrin and sense his self-doubt.

It was possible to secure victory though. The enemy were only three, and the magic of the ring was giving way.

When it did so, the vizier felt his own heartbeat begin to pound. Battle was fast approaching, and nothing said between the two groups would change that.

Castanuin saw his rival for the first time. He knew somewhat of him, but rumor was no substitute for reality. The man was strong in magic and sure of purpose. He had a weakness though. He felt mercy, and as the two druids spoke he tried to save Amrog.

It was noted. Mercy was a vulnerability, and if possible that might be used against him in the future. Amrog might kill him now, but Castanuin began to have doubts.

The fighting broke out. Drom moved with the natural-born grace of a predator. Every motion set him up for another strike, and soldiers died swiftly. How had he kept his arena skills for so long?

Again, Cadawn showed his failing. He used some of his strength to kill soldiers, which weakened him for the battle that must surely now play out. It would be a contest between druids, but instead of nurturing his power for that, he assisted his friends lest they suffer injury.

Castanuin concentrated on the girl. Was she really descended from Aroth?

Ariane certainly had power. That he could see, but while it was like that of the druids, either Court Druids or rebels, it was unlike too. He had not seen its like before.

What part would she play in all this? How could a dead god be resurrected?

It was not for him to fathom. Arofel had laid the charge on him to stop them, and that was all that mattered.

Amrog was not up to the task. He was about to be slain. Cadawn overmatched him, and that was about to play out.

The dream that was no dream unfolded before his eyes, and then it suddenly sharpened. Someone crept up behind Amrog.

With a violent blur the vision faded. Amrog was dead, and the vision lost, for now. Of all people it was the farmer the druid had recruited who had killed him. That was a surprise, and something to note. The man had managed to resist the warrior-spell.

Castanuin sat back and recomposed himself. It was not pleasant to be attached to someone by magic when they died. Yet slowly his breathing came back to normal, and he opened his eyes to his own room in his own palace.

Slowly, he felt better, and then he laughed. It was a joyous occasion. The loss of Amrog was nothing, but the trap he planned had now been set and would surely see his enemies killed and the desire of Arofel fulfilled.

He was not one to take chances though. Few plans survived contact with the enemy, so plans must come in waves. It was a lesson he had learned over long years.

Quickly he rang a bell and a nervous servant tentatively entered.

"Yes, my lord?"

"Tainlin has arrived?"

"Yes, my lord. He is waiting in the outer room as you instructed."

"Bid him enter. I am ready now."

He heard the druid shuffle first before he saw him. One leg had been maimed years ago, and Castanuin smiled at the thought of that. He had many druids to choose from for this mission, but Tainlin was perfect.

The man entered and bowed. "Sit, my old friend," Castanuin said. "We have much to discuss."

"At a guess, that means Amrog failed."

His old friend always had been shrewd.

"So it seems, but that game isn't quite played out. I need you. The task is dangerous. Will you accept it?"

The old druid grinned broadly. "If it is killing Isarn, you know I will."

The man had a grudge against the gladiator as great as his own. It was Isarn who had grievously injured his leg long ago in making his escape. Ruining a leg was not as bad as an eye, but they both hated him equally. Others had even more reason, but they were dead.

Castanuin put that tumultuous day out of his mind, with difficulty.

"Do it for both of us. Kill him, and it need not be fast. And the High Priestess. The rebel druid Cadawn is with them also."

The other man's grin grew wider. "Two questions. One, where are they? And two, I'm old enough to avoid pride. Isarn cannot be what he was, but he defeated us before. And now has allies. I cannot overcome them by myself. How many druids will you put under my charge for the task?"

The questions showed exactly why this man was the best option for the task. He was too old to think about becoming archdruid one day, so he had no ulterior motive. He just wanted to kill Isarn. And he knew his limitations and made no attempt to hide them. Amrog had been too sure of himself, and paid the price for it.

"I have pondered the old prophesies in light of the new information we have. Not least where Isarn was last located, and the direction he was heading. Go swiftly to Brandwil's Fortress and after that Brandwil's Seat. I believe they are heading to one or the other, though I may have better information for you later."

The old man nodded at that, but did not speak. He was waiting for his second question to be answered.

101

Castanuin sat back in his chair. He had given much thought to this, and he was confident in his final decision. He did not think he would regret it, but it was a granting of great power.

"You will go by yourself."

Tainlin raised an eyebrow but said nothing. His mind was swift, and he knew there must be more.

"I give you no druids to command, but I will give you a talisman of power instead."

As he spoke Castanuin drew forth from a pocket a small leather bag. He was tempted to undo the strings and look inside, but that was best avoided. The object held enormous magic, but he did not trust it. The archdruid before him had given it to him, and warned against its use. *It is for the time of prophecy only, if that should come during your leadership. Give it to a trusted druid, but disdain use yourself. All magic exacts a price, but this runs deeper than a sword stroke.*

For long years he had resisted the lure, and though the power of the talisman was great, what use was power if you were dead?

He handed the pouch to Tainlin. The druid felt the weight of the bag first, no doubt wondering what could be inside. Then he opened it, and spilled the contents onto his palm.

It was a single stone. Perfectly round, and a little smaller than a dove's egg. It was not white though. Mostly, it was black. It glistened like water coated by oil, shifting and moving and giving the impression of things contained within, not quite visible, trying to get out.

The stone was heavier than it seemed, though its weight was not constant. Nor its size. Both seemed mutable, though it was never possible to observe any transition.

Castanuin knew all this by long experiment. Many was the time he had held it thus, in his palm, fascinated by it, turning it to and fro for hours while the world went by ignored. Yet never succumbing to use it. He was one to heed warnings.

"It cannot be, surely?" Tainlin said. His voice was barely a whisper.

"It is."

All druids had heard stories of talismans like this. The elders, such as Tainlin, were permitted to study the lore regarding them. Of course, some lore was more secretive than others.

Nor was the lore comprehensive. In antiquity, some druids possessed stones such as this. But none now for hundreds of years. Or longer.

"It is a *faestone*," the vizier said. "What do you know of them?"

The other man clenched his fist around it. Perhaps he sensed the danger of studying it too long.

"Not much. I never read deeply of those passages in the lore books that mention them. They were not crafted by druids, but were gifts from creatures of faery. They hold strong magic. The magic is different for each user, as though the stone itself decides what is most needed."

"Or as though the stone draws out of the wielder something of their individual selves," Castanuin offered.

The stone was deadly dangerous. All gifts of faery were, for their magic was dangerous and the denizens of that realm capricious.

Tainlin glanced at him, quickly understanding what was meant.

"You mean a faestone draws power from the wizard who uses it?"

"Indeed. And that is not all. Even Arofel forbids the use of a faestone. It is said that after some use your powers get stronger. The stone becomes more puissant. It keeps drawing on the user, bringing forth more and more

103

strength. Sometimes more than is possessed. That can be deadly. Other stories say the more the stone is used, the more the creature of faery that gave it to humanity in the first place gains control over them, and can dominate their mind."

"Are such stories true? And if Arofel forbids their use, how can I invoke its power?"

Castanuin was in doubt. He knew the stories, and he knew what the previous archdruid had said. In truth though, he knew nothing for sure.

"You'll discover these things if you accept the task. I can offer no more than that. You have the chance to become an expert on faestones because I have not used it, nor, I think, any archdruid right back to the time of the Shadowed Wars. As for Arofel though, she has suggested this is a special circumstance."

That was a lie and a truth in one. He was not sure what Arofel thought on the matter. He knew she was doing all she was permitted to do to kill her enemies, and in the case of Aroth to ensure he could not be resurrected. Whether or not she would sanction the use of a faestone was another matter.

None of it was relevant though. Drom and the others yet lived, and they must be killed. If his first plan did not work, the faestone would become more than an option. It would be necessity, and in this matter it was his decision and not Arofel's. He possessed the stone, and he had sanctioned its use. Possession of a power gave the right to use, or withhold it.

"Do you accept the quest, benefits and risks both?"

It was more of an option than he would give to most druids. Tainlin was no fool though, and he was an old friend. If he died, or worse, so be it. He had the right to choose though.

The old man did not answer at once. Instead, he opened his fist and studied the stone. It seemed different now, black, and yet with a milky sheen to it that swirled like miniature clouds deep in the stone.

"I accept."

Castanuin let out a long breath. He did not trust anyone else with the stone. The man who sat opposite him was now more powerful. Indeed, more powerful than any druid who ever lived, with the exception, maybe, of the traitor Conhain.

"Good. There's another element to your quest. With the stone, we have a talisman of enormous power. We must also deprive the enemy of theirs, permanently. For even if the three of them are killed, who is to say others might not take their place, even if it took another thousand years?"

"And what is their talisman?"

"They seek it. You know the druid staff is broken. Cadawn searches for a replacement. If he yet lives when you find him, let him discover it first. Then kill him and bring it back. We will destroy it if we can, or better, turn it to our own uses."

"What talisman could be as great as the druid staff that was broken?"

As always, the old man's mind was sharp. Castanuin had chosen the wielder of the faestone wisely.

"I have not discovered that. Yet a staff is made of timber, and what tree produces wood sacred to the druids, and that might have magic of its own?"

The face of Tainlin was blank as he pondered that. Then slowly his eyes widened in shock.

"It cannot be. Surely?"

"We can hope not. But if indeed the staff comes from the Tree of Aroth, you now understand why I have given you the faestone. You *must* defeat our enemies, and retrieve their talisman."

The old man left then, limping out with a determined expression. He might be disabled of body, but that meant nothing. He was the single most powerful man to walk the realm.

What to do with him if he were successful was a problem though. He had no real ambition, and was too old to think about being archdruid. Yet if he possessed both the faestone and a second talisman of power, all the druids combined might not be able to control him.

15. A King of Old

The travelers had left the ring of standing stones behind them that afternoon. It was eerily quiet in the dark forest as though many eyes watched them. Perhaps they did, for this was a place of faery and Drom knew it without Cadawn saying so. There was a feel to such places that was not entirely welcoming but not hostile either.

A watch was set when they camped. Not for fear of the enemy pursuing them, for they had been vanquished, and the farmer, the only one remaining alive, had departed back toward his farm.

Drom hoped the man made it. It was a long way away now, and there were many dangers in the wild. In the end he had thrown off the shackles of fear and even the enchantment of the druid to assert his free will. It was no small accomplishment, and it was to be admired. The ill will that was between them had gone, and it was better that way.

The future lay ahead. And however dangerous it was for Castanuin it was more so for the three travelers. They had defeated the vizier for now, and had a chance to steal a march on him. With luck, they would retrieve the staff and move on to the next stage of the quest before ever the vizier could act against them.

They pressed through the strange land, desolate and broken. The forest was behind them now, and the rolling hills flattened. After some days the grass greened again, and though still a wild land the eeriness was gone.

"Where exactly are we?" Ariane asked.

Cadawn drew his horse to a halt and glanced around as though looking for landmarks. There was nothing special to see though.

"We're in the East March, and soon enough we should find Brandwil's Fortress."

They said no more then, and concentrated on traveling quickly. By the evening they had established a good camp on the crest of a slope. It was thick with trees, but only a small patch. Still, it offered good cover for their fire from prying eyes, if there were any at all in this abandoned land.

There was a spring near the crest, and they filled their water bags and let their horses drink freely. Cadawn had a knack for finding such places, and Drom wondered if it was experience at traveling that gave it or some form of magic. The druids, it was said, were one with the land and the land one with them.

The campfire blazed, having been stoked after dinner was cooked. The warmth and light it gave were comforting, and Drom liked it. He had lived in the city and the wild, and he would take the wild every time. It could be lonely though, but a good fire was company.

"Brandwil Fortress isn't far away," Cadawn told them. "We should reach it soon, if I learned my lessons well."

Drom smiled to himself at that. The druid had a sharp memory, and he was studious. He was one to *always* learn his lessons well.

"What was the truth about Brandwil?" Drom asked. "I know some of the legends, but what actually happened?"

The druid had been playing with a stick in the fire, poking and prodding, but he let it fall and shook his head.

"What do they teach you in the western schools these days? Obviously not much about the east."

Drom had always thought of Camlanta as one land, but he suddenly perceived the truth of Cadawn's words. History was taught by the victor, and once the realm had been several lands. It was the west that had grown and conquered it all. The east had been populated by those who had migrated, and they took their own history with them. Only the legends remained.

"I have heard the stories," Drom said. "He was a war leader during the elù-haraken. In the end, he was defeated. Not by the Dark though, but rather by treachery from those closest to him. Against the Dark, he won great victories."

The druid sighed. "It is always so, Drom. Heed my words well. The great are usually betrayed. The trusting are deceived by their friends. The Light fails just when it is about to shine brightest."

They were dark words. Drom had lived long enough to understand the truth in them though.

Cadawn went on. "Brandwil was a king, at least of sorts. He did not rule the realm of Camlanta, so we might call him only a chief, yet he had sub chiefs under him. At times in our past of great troubles a leader was chosen from among all the clans. The tribes bickered and fought and nurtured petty feuds among each other, but in times of peril they united, for a time, under one ruler. He was, for want of a better word, a war leader. He was the glue that held the eastern clans together. His title was Pendraig, in the dialect of the east."

It was a word that stirred Drom. He knew the legends. Only the great had ever been given that title, and none had held it long. The Camar were a capricious people, capable of the highest good but mostly falling short. Or maybe that was all peoples. Whatever the case, those who earned the title were heroes out of the past, almost godlike, and the stories about them echoed down the cold aisles of time for centuries. The fact that they had been overthrown at the height of their glory, one and all, only lent to their greatness rather than detracted from it.

"He fought many battles," Cadawn said. "Battle after battle, and won victory after victory. For a time, he alone held the Dark at bay."

"Until he was betrayed," Ariane said.

"Yes. He was betrayed. By his best friend, his wife and his nephew. But does it matter?"

Drom understood what the druid meant. Even now people talked about the time of Brandwil, a thousand years after his death. The nobility of his court, his example of sacrifice for service, and the prosperity of his realm amid the ineluctable tide of the Dark. That it was inundated in the end was not the point. That it had existed, however briefly, was the important thing. If it had existed once, it could exist again. It was a shining example of what should be striven for.

"After the betrayal there was a civil war among his people. In the end, he won that too, though it cost him his life. And then the wave of the Dark washed over the land, and would have destroyed it save for Aroth."

"It was the best of our people that migrated eastward," Ariane said. "At least that is the lore of the priestesses."

"Ours too," the druid said. "Even in our victory, when the Shadowed Wars were at last won, our people sowed the seed for evil. And it grew and prospered, for many that were left had fought on the side of Brandwil's enemies."

Drom felt a weight of regret upon him. How different the realm could have been. Even *should* have been. Humanity though had a habit of slipping into evil. Greed was at its root, and the thirst for power. He understood it, but he did not like it. Then again, he had never felt the temptation for he had never been in such a position. Would he be different from the kings of Camlanta, or the Court Druids, had he inherited the power they wielded? He hoped so, but he feared the opposite.

The fire was burning low. A nightbird swooped over the camp, and in the distance was the long, drawn out call of some bird he did not recognize.

"One last thing," Drom said. "The legend says, though gravely wounded in his final battle, Brandwil did not die. He was taken to a resting place, and there he sleeps yet waiting upon the darkest day of Camlanta. When it dawns, he will return to fight again."

Drom knew the answer. No man lived that long, enchanted sleep or otherwise, and it was a story to give people hope. That was all.

Even so, Cadawn, who was about to answer, paused. A faraway look entered his eyes, and Drom had the uncanny feeling the druid was not there at all. At least his mind was not.

"This is the twilight of Camlanta," the druid murmured after a while. "Many things are possible. The realm will sink into the Dark, or a new day will dawn. I cannot say which it will be, but my heart tells me you will soon discover the answer to your question."

It was not his heart that spoke, Drom knew. The druid had experienced some vision of the future. He was sure of it, but Cadawn would say no more and soon they slept.

As usual, Drom dreamed deeply. Nightmares were scattered among inconsequential figments of imagination, but they were not so bad as to cause him to wake in a cold sweat.

He did see a woman in his dreams though. Fair as she had been described in stories, for she was a creature of faery. Or so the stories claimed. Long was her hair and bright her eyes that glittered, but tragedy marked her features. Drom knew her, and knew it was but a dream. Every child in Camlanta could describe her. Gahranrir, wife of Brandwil.

The new day saw the travelers ride swiftly. The country was changing, and it was becoming fair again. The grass was green and the woods many, if small. Mostly they were of oak. Nor were they stunted. They grew tall and spread wide.

Just when Drom was beginning to like the landscape, it swiftly changed again.

"We're still in the Broken Lands," Cadawn said.

It grew worse rapidly. The grass dried up, and the trees thinned out and then disappeared. The horses churned dust as they walked forward, and the sun beat down harshly.

Once more they rode in single file with the druid in the lead. There seemed to be a road, but it was badly rutted and many obstacles lay over it. Rocks were frequent, and sometimes stones as large as a man were scattered before them.

Moving to the side was not much better. There were pits there, full of scummy water and the sound of insects chirping. Drom saw no frogs, but mosquitoes were plentiful even in daylight.

It was a lesson to him. Only a few miles away the land was fair. It was as it had been long ago. This was not new, where they were now. But it was not the natural state of Camlanta. Battles had been fought here, and magics that he could not conceive unleashed.

It could happen again. The powers of the world were stirring. The king and the vizier were acting, but they were only tools. Behind them was the shadow of the goddess Arofel, pushing, nudging, scheming.

Against that was Aroth. It was not the first time he wondered what powers a dead god could have. Some, maybe. The three travelers had come together on this quest, and, according to the Druid at least, that was prophesied. They were to resurrect a god. Had they come together by pure chance though?

And what would happen if Aroth really were resurrected? Would it start a conflict between Aroth and Arofel? Maybe other gods as well, and all of faery and humanity?

His blood ran cold. In trying to save the land, the three of them could be propelling it toward destruction. Looking around, he could see the results of battle unchecked and powers of magic unloosed without restraint.

And yet if Aroth were not returned to restore balance among the gods, then Camlanta was doomed as well.

It was too much to contemplate, and there were no answers to be had. He did not believe much in faith, yet maybe there were times when that was what was required.

The warrior in him had thought enough. He was no philosopher, but rather a man of action. What he needed most was information. Just at the moment, that related to their immediate destination.

"What can we expect at Brandwil Fortress and Brandwil's Seat?" he asked. The enemy druid was dead, but he knew the vizier and it was in just such a situation that he would set a trap.

"The fortress is a fortress," Cadawn answered. "It was his stronghold, but it would have been looted long ago of anything the migrating tribes had left behind. Supposedly it's still standing, that much I've been told by travelers. It's dilapidated though, and we must be careful there."

"And this supposed seat?"

"I know less of that. The story goes though, if you can believe it, that in times of trouble he went there to view his realm. It's in a high place, and he could survey much of his domain for enemies and activity. Probably he went there for peace and quiet too. Who knows?"

Drom did not like it. The more he considered it the more he thought both places would be perfect for a trap.

16. Captured

The travelers slowed down as they entered deeper into a dreary land. Previously, they could ride for a morning to cover the same distance that took two days where they were now.

It was not quite hill country, but there were many steep slopes and high ridges. The earth was blasted, and little grew on it. Mostly it was scree slopes and gulleys of sand. Here and there were slag heaps to relieve the monotony.

More dangerous were the fissures in the bedrock. Whatever dark forces had shaped this land set them running in zigzag directions. Some were empty and yawned into the depths of the earth. These would often necessitate backtracking a half hour or so to find a new path. Others were filled with rank water. They too could not be crossed.

"Magic is pitiless," Cadawn muttered as they rode.

Drom knew what he meant. In the books of lore he had long ago read magic exerted a price, or it came at a cost. It was not easy to acquire, and it was harder to use. He saw the effect of that all around him. Magic was like a live thing, and once unleashed it ran toward unintended consequences.

Even so, there was more going on here. This was intended, for beyond doubt some of the great battles of the Shadowed Wars had been fought here. Magic was a weapon, loosed to destroy and kill. If it had done this to the land, and remained so starkly visible a thousand years later, what must it have done to the armies that fought those battles?

115

Drom was a lone warrior rather than a soldier, but his heart went out to those who had fought. Even to the enemy. Like most armies, the soldiers likely did not choose to fight. They would rather be at home ploughing fields, or hammering at an anvil, or whatever their trade was. They would have been conscripted and made to fight by their leaders.

It was the way of the world. The old led, and they sent young men to die for their ideas. Even in the Shadowed Wars, where the primal forces of all Alithoras combated one another, and battling armies of men were just one piece on the gameboard, it must have been so.

There were always men like the vizier. Shrewd and ambitious. Greedy for power, knowledge or fame. He should know. Fame had been his own weakness.

He glanced at Ariane. If she were really his daughter, he could not tell her about all his life. His face reddened with shame, and he felt the heat of it.

They crested a rise and looked around them from their vantage. All they saw was desolation.

"According to legend," Cadawn said, "one of the great battles was fought here. You have seen the burial mounds near Car Sagoth, but in truth that was a minor conflict. Here, vast armies contended. Men against men. Elves against goblins. Dwarves. Creatures of faery. Wizards, druids and sorcerers."

"And dragons," Ariane added. "Not just a few, but scores of them. Only they could unleash such destruction."

Cadawn sighed. "Yes, dragons too. The land still feels the heat of their fire, and the torture of their breath."

Drom was looking at the druid as he spoke, and it seemed as though he were in actual pain. If the connection between druid and land was as strong as stories claimed, it would be no surprise.

116

The Court Druids did not have that though. More and more Drom was beginning to appreciate how different the two kinds of druids were from each other.

It was hot. The heat of the sun beat down, and the barren earth reflected it upward again. They drank deeply, and then pushed ahead.

It was a difficult trail downhill. The fissures were many, and out of the very rock a dark substance oozed.

"Tar," Cadawn said. "Stay clear of it."

Drom had read of it, but never seen it. The horses did not like the smell, and it was easy to avoid. That took time though, and they had covered little ground before the westering sun began to cast long shadows.

They found no water, at least that was drinkable, and rode ahead until the sun set. Then they were forced to shelter in a hollow, for a northerly wind picked up, coming down from the Tainglint Mountains, and the temperature plummeted swiftly.

They ate a meagre meal, sparing their food. But especially they spared their water. Supplies were running low, and the horses got the most of it.

"If I'm right," Cadawn said, "we should soon leave this barren place and approach the fortress. It was spared much of the fighting, and the landscape is wholesome there, and we'll find running water to drink."

It was a quiet camp. No one felt much like talking, and their spirits were low. They soon went to sleep.

Ariane took the first watch. She sat upon a boulder at the rim of the hollow, and Drom watched her a while before he slept. She was so much like her mother, and just like her mother was surprising.

It was strange to think of her as a high priestess. Certainly she could be a little preachy at times, though she mostly avoided that. She could be stern sometimes, and at others easy going. She was quick to laugh but thoughtful.

Her mind was as sharp as the vizier's, but she had a great store of mercy and compassion. She wished to hurt no one, but in defense she did not hesitate to wield a blade. He hoped she really was his daughter, and if so, he could not be more proud of her.

Sometime a little before midnight Drom woke from an unpleasant dream. A cold sweat was on his face, and there was no warmth from the fire. He saw Cadawn take over the watch, sitting on the same boulder, but it was very dark now and the light of the fire dwindled to near nothing.

Ariane stoked the fire a little, then wrapped herself in cloak and blankets and lay down near the horses. Drom closed his eyes, and sleep came again swiftly.

Just as swift, it seemed, he felt a nudge against his shoulder and Cadawn woke him. It was his turn to watch, and no matter that it seemed he had only just gone to sleep again the stars had moved substantially. It was now that quietest period of night, long after midnight yet still a good while before dawn, where the land held the hushed promise of a new day but it had not come yet.

"Anything unusual?" Drom whispered.

The druid shook his head. "I thought I saw something move in the shadows, but it was probably just a fox."

Drom climbed up to the perimeter of the hollow. He did not sit down on the boulder immediately, but let his eyes adjust to the darkness, staring out into the shadows.

He was still a little sleepy, so he walked around the hollow a few times, and when he was satisfied that he would not doze he sat down on the boulder. It was the highest point and should have given a good view, but the night was very dark and a bank of clouds rolled over the sky to block out even the starlight.

His mind turned to the vizier. Once, they had been friends, at least as much as that kind of man ever had any. Now hatred connected them.

Drom knew no matter what happened, his old friend, now his oldest living enemy, would never give up. Too much injury had been done, both to his eye and his pride, to allow that. And Ariane added urgency to the situation.

What would the vizier do though? *Always seek the unexpected action.* That was what the vizier himself used to say, and Drom could hear his voice after all these long years as though they had last spoken yesterday. Those words related to court infighting and ambition though, not the life and death struggle that this had become. Still, his methods of operation would not have changed. They were good, which was why Drom had adopted them himself. They had served him well in his decades of exile and hiding from the assassins, soldiers and druids constantly seeking him.

He glared into the dark night, but saw nothing. Even so, an uneasy feeling came over him. Thinking of the vizier always did that to him.

The feeling persisted though. He went perfectly still, except for his right hand that eased down toward the hilt of his sword. He did that slowly, and he tried to pierce the dark with his eyes.

It was to no avail. He could see nothing, and maybe it was just anxiety. It often crept over a man on watch duty, or a lone man out in the wild.

Even as he began to breathe easy again, he heard the slightest of noises. It was close. Too close. He began to jump away from the boulder and yell, but at the same time a dim shadow swayed upright near him. There was a whizzing sound and then something crashed into his head. A darkness more complete than the night fell.

Drom swam in a world of shadows. It was not a dream, nor yet was he awake. It was as though his mind were underwater, and he tried desperately to reach the surface. Some urgency drove him, but he did not know what.

Consciousness smote him like a blow. His head throbbed, and he felt a trickle of blood there. His arms were tied behind his back, and the rope was tight. Worse, Cadawn and Ariane were bound too, and they stood near him, surrounded by a group of shadowy forms. One of them had Drom's own sword girded at his waist, and white hot anger rose up in Drom like a towering inferno. He strained at his bonds, but they did not break.

For his troubles he was kicked in the head, and he nearly passed out again.

"Easy!" one of the figures said harshly. His accent was strange and his voice guttural. "Plenty of time for that later! For now, we march! Get moving. Move!"

Drom felt rough hands on him, and he was hauled to his feet. They began to march, and for the first time he could see clearly.

They were captured, but not by soldiers. Not of the King of Camlanta anyway. These were goblins. Goblins from the old stories of faery, and elugs in legends of the Shadowed Wars. Servants of the Dark, and creatures of evil.

He understood what had knocked him out. Some of them carried slings, and no doubt a rock had hit him. He was lucky to be alive.

Or not. Being captured by goblins meant torture and death. At the least slavery in their underground mines, which came to the same thing in the end. Worse, it was his fault. He had been the one on watch and failed to see the attack coming. There were at least a score of them, but they were hard to keep track of. They were smaller than men, and their skin was swart, and their clothes, what little they wore, was dull also.

Yet they were well armed. Many had the curved swords of their kind, famous in tales, but some had straight swords, some axes, and all a knife sheath belted to them. Most had several.

It was a mismatch of weapons coming from no central smithy. Likely they had been taken from travelers over the years.

Ariane stumbled, and a goblin pushed her forward roughly so that she nearly fell again. Rage flooded Drom. He would kill them all. But he controlled the swell of raw emotion. Time for that later. For now, he must think of a plan and execute it swiftly. Once they were underground they might be separated, and then things would be impossible.

What could he observe that might help? Ariane had power, but she had not used it. He must be ready for it when it came. It was the same with Cadawn. He still wore the hathlinden on his forearms. Clearly the goblins had no idea what they were, but the druid had magic, enhanced by the hathlinden, and that was promising.

Why had neither acted yet? Drom was not sure. Perhaps they merely waited until he recovered from his blows so he could assist.

If he were to do that though, it would help to have his hands free. That was his first task, and he began to work on the rope that bound him. He tensed and swelled muscles, then relaxed. Given time, he just might work free. Not likely though.

He could still kick. The goblins did not know he was a gladiator, and in the arena he had learned the uses of every weapon, and strikes of hand, foot, grappling, headbutts and how his entire body could be used as a weapon. One way or another, he would be ready when the time came.

What else could he observe? He studied the goblins as they marched. They went with great speed, as though they were in a hurry. That might mean they feared being out in the open, or being caught out in the open by someone.

The way they spoke seemed to back that up. Their voices were guttural, and they conversed tersely now and then in their own language. But not very much, and when they did they kept their voices low. It was like they feared to be seen or heard, and that implied enemies.

He kept working on his bonds. That was his main task, but he knew there was not a lot of time left. Goblins dwelled underground, and seldom went abroad during daylight hours. And already the stars seemed a little paler and the eastern horizon was beginning to gray. Whatever must be done must be done soon.

Drom thought of his youth. He had survived so much in the arena, and afterward when pursued by the king's soldiers and the vizier's druids. He did not intend to die at the hands of goblins.

The band of elugs led them down a steep gulley. The rocks beneath their boots crunched, and the clatter of their passing was loud. They moved all the faster.

Fame and wealth were fleeting things, and Drom felt it now more than ever. He had gold enough to buy a throne, but what good would it do him now? Now, as always, it came down to the courage of his heart and the wit of his mind. And his friends.

If he lived though, he would give much of that gold to Ariane. He had stashes in the countryside in various places, along with food and weapons. He had accounts with merchants, though not in his true name. Investments were many, and money was always coming in from them, again held by the merchants. Probably Ariane would have no better use for it than he did though. He had no wish to buy a throne, and she had no desire to be a queen.

They came up out of the gulley, and it was lighter. The goblins halted a few moments, and then carried on. They marched even faster, and they seemed anxious.

The one who had Drom's sword was larger than most, nearly as large as Drom himself. He was marked for death though.

Suddenly, he stopped and listened, the troop doing likewise. In that moment Drom finally worked his hands free.

17. Even We Know Your Name

The predawn gray was sparked to life with bright flares.

With the flares came battle cries. The voices were harsh and guttural, and the words were in a strange tongue, but it was nothing like that of the goblins.

"Dwarves!" Cadawn cried.

Drom saw them clearly then. There were a half dozen, two with lanterns in one hand of strange design that burned brightly. All with axes. And those tools of death fell among the goblins like a team of woodcutters in a forest of saplings.

Surprise was on their side. Yet they were badly outnumbered. Drom strode forward, and with a mighty blow of his fist he felled the goblin that had taken his sword and now dared raise it in battle. The goblin crumbled, but it was temporary.

Despite the blow the creature surged up, and Drom smote him again. This time the goblin fell all the way to the ground, and remained still. Swiftly Drom retrieved his sword, and the thrill of it in his hand again ran through him.

The goblins were turning on their prisoners trying to kill them. Fire flashed from Cadawn's hands, and Drom saw they were free. Magic had burned the ropes away.

One of the creatures was trying to stab Ariane. A nimbus of white light suddenly glowed all around her, but though the creature was wary it still stalked her.

Drom hewed off its head, and then he spun around. A dwarf was fighting beside him. Two goblins hacked at him with their curved blades, and he retreated.

The sword was light in Drom's hand, and the joy of battle on him. His pent up fury from earlier suddenly burst forth like a storm, and he ran one of the goblins through and stabbed at the other just as the axe of the dwarf bit into him also.

In the twilight the dwarf grinned fiercely at him, and then both were away and leaping into the rest.

The battle did not last long. Most of the goblins were killed quickly, and even as the sun sprang up over the horizon and bathed the land in a faint yellow glow the last of the creatures fled.

They did not get far. There were three of them, and two fell to thrown daggers. The third stumbled, and then raced away.

"After him!" ordered the dwarf Drom had helped before. He seemed to be their leader, and a younger dwarf, still bearded but seemingly swifter of foot than the others, raced away in pursuit.

The rocky ridge on which they stood was red with blood, and dead bodies lay scattered grotesquely over it. Even so, Drom's friends were all alive, and he breathed a sigh of relief.

They assessed one another, swords and axes dripping blood, the glow of power about Ariane and the magic of the druid fading.

"Well met, korrig warriors. Your help was timely." The druid bowed to them.

At that, the dwarves seemed surprised. "You know our name in our own speech?"

Drom was surprised too. There were different names for dwarves in all the old stories, but he had never heard that one before. Yet it was a name that fitted the way they spoke.

"It's not the first time that I've met your people. I had heard some lived here, but I have met your brethren in the Tainglint Mountains."

The korrig leader scratched his beard, and then remembering his manners bowed in return, and it was a low bow, yet done with grace for such a sturdily built person. Drom guessed none of them were over five feet high, but he had seen them fight and knew they swung those axes with strength enough to shame any gladiator he had ever seen.

"You have the look about you of a druid. We thought as much, yet you have no staff and that troubled us."

"Ah, yes. Well, my staff was broken in a fight with a gortha."

At that word the dwarves made a sign against evil. It was one that Drom had seen often, but he wondered to see it done by dwarves. He remembered though, according to the books he had read in the vizier's palace, that humanity had learned much from such folk in the distant past. The sign was likely just one thing of many.

"My name is Cadawn, and I'm at your service and in your debt."

The dwarf leader looked at him long and hard. "We have heard of you. You're the Archdruid of Car Sagoth. We have little chance to speak to our richer brothers in the Tainglint Mountains, but they have spoken of you, and to all dwarves the loyal druids are revered." He bowed again.

"We druids still revere Conhain ourselves, who killed the dragon Rah-essen long ago and revenged the dwarves he had killed. So both our peoples are bound by that great deed."

The dwarf leader wiped the blood off his axe on the body of a goblin.

126

"My name, in your speech, is Gorik. I'm a captain of a band of us that patrol these lands. Our people are few and poor here, but this is where we've dwelt a long time. And there's constant war between us and the elugs."

The dwarves were gathering in close, listening intently to all that was said. One of them however, at a sign from Gorik, kept watch a little distance away. The goblins were beaten, but nothing had been heard yet of the one that had fled. If it lived, it might bring a greater band down upon them.

Cadawn introduced the dwarf leader to Ariane, and he gave her the proper title of High Priestess of Aroth. At this the dwarves were amazed.

"You honor us, lady," Gorik said. "Our land is humble, and so too our people, but we still remember the old ways. Will you bless us?"

Ariane smiled. "Of course." One by one she laid a gentle touch upon their shoulders, and she muttered a prayer as she did so, and then they kissed the back of her hand.

It was not a ceremony Drom had seen before. Few were those who publicly practiced any rituals of the Cult of Aroth, but it was better tolerated in the arena. He had seen nothing like it there, either.

The dwarves seemed renewed, and their eyes shone and a peace was upon them vastly different from the anger of battle just moments ago.

Cadawn then gestured toward Drom. "This is a gladiator from the king's arena. His name there was Isarn the Invincible."

A hush fell over the dwarves, and there was a look of great respect to them. Gorik bowed yet again.

"The same Isarn," he said, "who fought more in the arena than any other, and lived? The same Isarn who slew Court Druids and gave the Archdruid his injury?"

Drom was surprised. "You know of me?"

Gorik laughed, and it was a deep rolling sound full of mirth.

"Know of you? Who in the land, be they man or dwarf or elf does not? You're a legend, and you have not died to earn the title, which most need to do before their fame grows as grandly as yours."

"Well, I haven't died, but I've been so well hidden that I might as well have been."

"But you have not, and we rejoice at that."

The dwarves all around gave a cheer, though Drom noticed it was not overly loud. Even the lookout did, but he did not take his attention from watching the countryside round about.

Drom had heard that dwarves were fond of human warriors, for they respected courage and skill at arms, whomever possessed it. They were a warrior people.

The lookout gave a low whistle, and the dwarves were suddenly alert, their axes in their hands. It was only the young dwarf returning though.

"What happened?" Gorik asked.

"He got away from me. He slipped down a hole less than half a mile away. It was little more than a fissure in a cliff face, but I guess it was an entrance to some goblin tunnel. I did not think I had much chance of killing him in there, in the dark, had I pursued him. Likely I would have been killed by him or his friends. So I returned."

Gorik considered that. "You showed good judgement. Goblin tunnels are no place for a lone dwarf, and now we have proof enough that more of them are likely close by. It's time to move on, and swiftly."

The dwarf leader turned to Cadawn. "We must leave, and perhaps for your safety you should come with us. It's clear though that something eventful is starting in the wider world beyond our lands. We've seen signs, but none greater than the Archdruid of Car Sagoth, the High Priestess of Aroth and Isarn the Invincible traveling together through our realm. Will you not tell us what is afoot?"

18. Expect the Unexpected

Cadawn hesitated, and Drom understood why. The korrig warriors had helped them, maybe even saved their lives. And dwarves, though they could be dour and grim according to legend, always fought on the side of Light. Even so, secrecy in the quest for the staff was paramount.

The druid looked at Ariane. She gave a slight but definite nod. Then Cadawn glanced at Drom. He hesitated, being ever cautious, but these were people who had risked their lives to help. Although it must also be acknowledged that there seemed to be a long feud between dwarves and goblins, and they may have ambushed them regardless of any prisoners.

He nodded too. Once his mind was made up, he would take the consequences. The korrig might even be able to help.

"Many things are indeed afoot," Cadawn said. "The druid staff that Conhain himself bore was broken fighting the gortha."

At that news the dwarves muttered into their beards. Even Gorik seemed dismayed, but he quickly recovered.

"Ill news indeed. You said before that your staff was broken, but I had not realized it was *that* staff. It is said it held great power."

"It was a talisman of strength," Cadawn answered. "Yet the world moves on and the ancient days pass. New days are coming, and against this Conhain laid plans. He foresaw the breaking of the talisman. Nor is that as bad as it seems."

As the druid spoke he raised his arms and the silver bands upon them shone with a ruddy glow in the early morning light.

"Behold! The staff was an object of the druids, and many throughout Camlanta revered it, but the true power was in these. The very same hathlinden that Conhain retrieved from the hoard of Rah-essen, whom he slew."

Gorik looked sharply at the bands. "I see them now. It is told that the elves crafted them, and I see their skill and style. It is different from dwarf work, but of old the dwarves and elves shared knowledge of smithcraft. What you wear on your arms is worth more than all the gold in the cities of men."

"More indeed, and as the bands were added to the druid staff by Conhain, so too must I find a new staff, and a new talisman will be made."

The druid lowered his arms and hesitated momentarily, then went on.

"That is our quest. A new druid staff, but not any timber will do."

The dwarves gathered round closely, listening. Their beards were dark. Their eyes glinted. Legends said they enjoyed a fight, and they understood a lifechanging battle was playing out now. The Archdruid of Car Sagoth was on a quest, and against him were arrayed the forces of the Dark.

"There are few timbers that can withstand the power of magic. Oak is one, and many a druid of old used it, and though the Court Druids have forsaken the tradition of staves, we at Car Sagoth have not. Yet the staff of the archdruid must be stronger than even oak."

The korrig warriors barely breathed. They understood magic better than humanity, and Drom could see their intent faces as they tried to reason their way through what would be better than oak.

131

"Though Conhain is famed throughout the land," Cadawn said, "few people know much of what he actually did. He was a seer though, and foresaw much of what would be, and against the dark powers that were growing ascendant in this land, he laid plans. Talismans he crafted, each fitting for its purpose even if he would be long dead before the time of their use dawned."

Even Drom, who knew what was coming, felt excitement. Conhain was a figure of remote legend, yet he was a living, breathing person. He had planned for this time, and fought the Dark as he could in his own. He was now becoming real, becoming more than a story, and his courage was all the more to be respected. He had devoted his life to the winning of a battle that would be fought after he was dust and history had nearly swallowed him.

"One of those talismans," Cadawn nearly whispered, "was a staff. It was made from no ordinary timber. Our lore says the Tree of Aroth itself called to him, and he went to it, and from a limb of the tree on which the god was slain, from the tree that absorbed the dead god's blood, he made the staff we seek. But that is not all."

The dwarves stirred, and a ripple of awe ran through them.

"Know this! It is not just the staff we quest for. The talisman is to aid us on a greater task still."

"What is that?" Gorik said, but by the look of wonder on his face he had begun to realize what that might be.

"The time of the resurrection of Aroth is come! The Dark seeks to stop us, but whether or not it will prevail, or the forces of Light, even Conhain did not know. The staff will be power against the Dark though, and the three of us must go on these quests and do what must be done, or fall by the wayside. Yet all the free folk of Camlanta must fight also, in their way. Dark days are coming, and the powers of faery stir. So too the gods. Prepare yourselves for war, but pray for peace. If Aroth prevails, you will have it. If Arofel ascends, the Dark will engulf us all!"

The korrig warriors did a strange thing then. They struck the blades of their axes with the hilts of their daggers and they voiced the battle cry of their ancestors that no doubt had resounded in the Shadowed Wars themselves. A clatter of weapons went up, and a tumult of voices. Even so, they were careful not to be too loud. Especially since the last goblin had survived.

Gorik looked fierce. His eyes smoldered. His beard was stiff. And there was a determination in him more enduring than stone. The dwarves were smaller than men, yet still renowned as fighters. Drom had never faced one in the Arena, and he was suddenly glad of that.

"We have discussed what we may in the time given to us," the dwarf leader said. "This is a dangerous place, and we must leave. Already we have over lingered. Come back to our halls where we can talk in safety, and not every crevice around us might have a tunnel behind it full of elugs."

"Alas," Cadawn answered. "Time presses us too. The vizier will not have forgotten us I think. The druid he sent against us and the gortha roused from faery-sleep have failed. We must try to get ahead of him on our quest, for he will already have sent something else against us."

"It's a long way for such news to travel to Camalduin."

"Yet such news might be guessed, or feared, and acted on anyway. And the druids can speak over the vast miles. We must be gone, and swiftly. The road ahead of us is long. The sooner we start the less evil we may find ahead of us."

Gorik bowed. "It must be so. Remember then our people, as we will remember you. And know that the prayers of the korrig will be with you. Not as strong as steel axes, perhaps, but if Aroth can hear, not without power either."

The dwarf leader gave a signal to his warriors, and they made preparations to depart. The watchman joined them, and orders were given for the manner of their marching.

When all was readied, Gorik approached the druid again.

"Even the korrig have heard of this vizier, this false archdruid. You're right to be wary of him. All our soothsayers see shadows about him, dark and impenetrable. The hand of Arofel is over him, and the king. Be wary of both of them, and expect the unexpected. We must go swiftly now to our humble halls, but is there any favor we can grant before we part?"

Cadawn rubbed his chin. "One, if you are able. I'm not sure of this land. I haven't traveled here before, but I must find Brandwil Fortress swiftly. Can you spare us a guide to show us the way?"

The rising morning light flooded the land, and the korrig warriors cast long shadows.

"I can spare one. The path you must take brings you close to strongholds of the elugs though, so the way is dangerous. Are you sure you must go there?"

Cadawn seemed in doubt. "The druid prophecies are less clear than they could be. Firstly, that's the nature of what a seer sees. Secondly, Conhain was wary of betrayal or accident. So the trail he laid down for us is deliberately obscured in places lest the enemy learn of it. I cannot be sure Brandwil Fortress is the place we seek, but I know we must go there."

"Very well." Gorik moved back among his warriors and spoke briefly to them in quiet tones. Drom saw surprise on their faces at one point, though he did not hear what was said, then the dwarf leader returned, and the young warrior who had pursued the goblin was by his side.

"It would be better if we all went with you. There's unrest in this land. Evil things stir that have not been seen for long years. And the old wounds of the earth rumble underground. It cannot be though."

Gorik glanced at his young companion. "I must bring news swiftly to my king, both of our fight with the elugs and the news you've brought us. He'll need to ponder it all and take counsel from the elders. There are few of us to spare, for we may yet be attacked, but young Kentanos here has volunteered to share your own dangers for a while and guide you. According to the king's ban though, none of our folk are permitted to leave the realm without permission. He mistrusts the wider world, and he may be right to do so. So Kentanos must return when he has set you upon the proper path."

Cadawn nodded. "I understand, and it's more than enough." He turned to the young korrig warrior and offered him his hand. "Traveling companions it is, then. And I thank you for agreeing to be our guide."

The young dwarf pulled up his hood. "After failing to slay the elug, it was the least I can do. I may yet have a chance to redeem myself."

Swiftly then the two groups parted under the rising sun, and they said farewells and disappeared in different directions.

Kentanos immediately took the lead, hood up, hand on the haft of his axe carried in a belt loop, and with his gaze falling from side to side as he carefully assessed the land. Clearly, the dwarves thought that the goblins were stirred up and that even if they did not like daylight they might still attack.

He led them quickly, and for the most part over hard rock that left little sign of their passing.

Cadawn offered the dwarf to ride with him, but he just grinned and shook his head.

"I prefer two feet to four, and have no fear. I'll keep up with the horses. They'll tire before I do."

Drom did not think that statement an idle boast. The endurance of the dwarves was legendary, and many a tale told of feats that seemed unlikely yet the storytellers claimed as true.

Despite the fears of the dwarves, they traveled through the day and saw no sign of goblins. Perhaps those who had received warning from the lone goblin to escape truly shunned the daylight. Or feared the dwarves. Or, just maybe, there were not a great many of them. None of those things seemed overly likely though.

Drom considered it possible that Gorik's band might have been followed and attacked, and that was why he and his companions had seen nothing. If so, he feared for the korrig warriors. Yet they knew this land and were wary. They would not be ambushed, and if pursued by goblins he had faith they would outdistance them and perhaps spring their own trap when they reached the proximity of their underground halls.

The travelers rested briefly at midday. The sun beat down from above, and eagles soared in the currents of warm air. Yet as the afternoon drew on, and the travelers pushed forward again, dark clouds gathered on the horizon.

"I don't like the look of that," Kentanos said.

Cadawn shaded his eyes and studied the clouds. "We have nothing to fear from a little rain, if it comes. Danger gathers around us now worse than any storm on the horizon. It will unleash soon. It is destiny at work, and even gods may fall before such a tempest."

They were dark words, and the druid did not say which gods would fall and which would rise. That was a problem for the future though. Right now, Drom agreed with the dwarf. Rain was uncomfortable for any traveler, and he did not look forward to it.

19. Secret Ways

It rained that afternoon, and the downpour was heavy. Slopes turned to mud and paths became streams. Drom felt gloom descend upon him, and he did not like it.

For how many centuries had it rained like this? And yet despite it so few things grew in this land. Such were the consequences of a struggle for power in which magic was the chief weapon.

They camped on a high ridge early that night, for travel had become nearly impossible. Yet, despite the poor weather, they lit no fire. Probably they could not get one going anyway. Firewood was sparse at best, and now it was wet. Most of all though, Kentanos was wary of goblins. The travelers were already exposed at the top of a ridge, and a light would only serve as a beacon to draw eyes to them.

There were a few rumbles of thunder in the distance, and the sky was lit at times by lightning. The storm soon passed on though, and all that remained were some brief showers.

"We could be stuck here all tomorrow," Drom said. "Nowhere is safe to ride when all the land is mud."

"We will see," Kentanos said. "When it rains here the earth turns to mud swiftly because there is little grass. For the same reason, it dries out swiftly too. I think by midmorning we'll be on our way again."

The dwarf spoke little. He seemed to be at ease among them, but dwarves were renowned in stories for their fierceness in a fight and their closed-mouthed attitude with strangers.

As always, they set a watch that night. Ariane took the first turn, and she pulled her hood up against the chill air and took her position on a little hillock nearby.

The rain diminished, and a wind blew up out of the west. By the time Drom took his turn as watch, the clouds were rolling back to reveal bright stars.

Dawn showed them a bright sun but a wet landscape. Tattered clouds littered the sky, but they were streaking away even as the travelers looked out over the land.

"What do you think?" Cadawn asked the dwarf.

"Good and bad things. The rain will have covered our tracks getting here. When we leave though, we'll leave a trail a goblin, both drunk and blind, could follow."

As the korrig warrior spoke he stepped out from their camp a little, testing the ground. It was stony where they had slept, but nearby his heavy boots were leaving deep impressions.

"Three hours," he said. "The sun is up and the wind is blowing. It'll be dry enough by then for travel, if not sooner."

They spent the time talking quietly, except the dwarf. He said little unless asked, but he was growing accustomed to their company. Of them all, he spoke least to Ariane. He seemed to be in awe of her, and it was clear the dwarves held great reverence for Aroth.

It was humanity that had changed. They had forgotten the old ways, or abandoned them. Worse, they had adopted new ways, the ways introduced to them by the corrupt kings of the land, and behind the kings a long line of viziers. Likely enough, thought Drom, most of them were of a kind with the current one. Shrewd, seemingly affable when things went well or it suited, and scheming cauldrons of evil ready to spill a brew of death and darkness over the people whenever it suited.

139

But who was he to judge? He had killed men in the arena for gold, and to entertain crowds, and worst of all because of the thrill of victory.

It was well before midday when they started their journey again. Looking out from their vantage, they saw no sign of goblins, or any movement at all. As the sun heated the wet earth though, the air felt steamy.

Kentanos found the firmest path he could. His heavy boots sank somewhat into the earth, but for the most part he moved swiftly and lightly over the quickly drying ground. The horses churned things up more, but they had no difficulty.

They rested at midday. Again the korrig warrior chose a place that offered a good view of the surrounding countryside. And he stood at the highest point and looked around in all directions while the others prepared a meal.

"Anything out there?" Drom asked when the warrior returned and began to eat.

"Nothing. I trust our safety all the less because of that though."

No one argued with him. They felt it too. There could be eyes all around them, watching. It was a landscape that offered little in the way of opportunity to hide.

"Just because you don't see them," Kentanos said, referring to the goblins, "doesn't mean they aren't there. While they normally shun the daylight hours, that doesn't mean they're incapable of marching under the sun. Still less that they don't have watchers posted in the last place you'd look. And if we've been seen, they may send a band against us in the night."

It was not a comforting thought. They had already been captured once, and a second time around they may not be so lucky. There was nothing to do though but pass through the land as swiftly as possible, and keep their guard up.

When night fell, they kept traveling. It was better to ensure that if they had been seen then at least the place of their nighttime camp was not marked.

It was late in the evening by the time they stopped. The land had long since dried out from the rain, but they found a good stream where they watered the horses and replenished their own supplies.

Dinner was cold and sparse. They had received some supplies from the korrig, yet they had a long way to travel and eked out their rations accordingly. No one could say when next they would be passing by a town and in a position to buy food.

Kentanos seemed oblivious to the lack of fire and the cold meal. He ate contentedly, though remained his usual quiet self.

Cadawn, the most talkative of them all, sat on a flat rock and traced his fingers over the hathlinden. Left and right, by turns. Drom could almost read his thoughts. The quest for the staff was a great responsibility to him. The old talisman that Conhain himself had borne was destroyed. He would not be the druid who failed to obtain the replacement that was prophesied.

Ariane, less talkative than Cadawn but always joyful, brooded in the shadows. Hers was a greater responsibility than Cadawn's. He must replace a staff. A talisman of magic it might be, but it was still a staff. She, on the other hand, must resurrect a god. One, if the stories were true, she was descended from.

Drom believed the stories. She had power. Of that there was no doubt. Yet it was of a different kind than any he had seen the court druids use, and now the druids of Car Sagoth in turn.

How did one resurrect a god? Drom did not know where to even start trying to answer such a question. She would be thinking of it though.

He gazed into the night. What was his true part in all this? He did not belong here. He was just an escaped gladiator. Just an old man with regrets.

All he could hope for was redemption. He would protect Ariane with his life, and she would need it. He knew the vizier as the others did not, and that man would never give up or relent. He would keep pushing at them in different ways, and always do the unexpected. There was no way to plan against that.

They passed a quiet night. There was no indication of being followed, nor any sign of life anywhere in this empty land. Kentanos grew more agitated.

"It's not normal," he said. "We should have seen goblins by now. They infest this area. Even if they did not attack us, we should have seen some scouts or messengers, especially at dawn or dusk. Something is happening."

Drom did not like it. All his life he had learned from those who knew a subject better than him. The key was listening to those who truly knew what they were doing rather than just said they did. In the arena, that was easy. The loudmouths were soon killed. The survivors had much to teach.

It was not that much different here though. The korrig warriors and goblins were, essentially, at war with one another. Kentanos was young, at least by dwarf standards, but he was alive. He knew what he was doing, and if he was worried there was reason for it.

The countryside began to change the next day. The slopes grew steeper, and they climbed them. It was hard going, on the horses and the dwarf, but Kentanos kept up without difficulty as he had promised.

The steepness was not the only change. Trees had been rare before, and grasses sparse. Where there were scattered tufts, they were mostly withered and brown. Yet now trees were more common, and the grass, if not green, was not as dry and desolate.

"We come near the end of the Broken Lands," the dwarf said. "And near the end of the korrig realm."

It was noon when they saw at last what Kentanos had long feared.

"Down," hissed the dwarf.

They dismounted immediately, and gazed in the direction he was fixed on himself, eyes fierce and fists clenched.

It was a column of goblins. So much for what legends said, thought Drom, that they shunned sunlight. This group, at least twenty strong, marched a mile or so away to the east in broad daylight. The more he looked though, the more he realized how much they hurried, and how they were hunkered down as they hastened, backs bent and heads dropped low.

The area around the travelers was treeless, but it was not high. Kentanos and the others sunk down into some dried grasses, and peered above the tips. Yet the horses would be visible to any goblin with a keen eye. There was no place to hide them.

"Keep the mounts still," Cadawn said. "Any movement will surely give us away."

The goblins trekked forward at a rapid pace. Because they kept their heads low, or perhaps by good fortune, none of them saw the horses, and soon the troop was lost to sight.

"That was close," Kentanos said. "It was what Gorik feared as well. The goblins are active, and have been so for weeks. It's rare to see so many in broad daylight though."

"The shadow of evil stretches forth its hand to block the Light," Cadawn said. "No doubt, throughout Camlanta, creatures of the Dark stir, and grow stronger.

They sense battle is coming. It may even be that they are roused against us."

They rode ahead carefully then. What cover there was, they used. Mostly this meant avoiding cresting themselves on ridges and staying to the lower lying land.

This slowed them down. The ground was still moist in these places, and they also offered terrain where an ambush could more easily be set.

Kentanos was wary, as well he should be. Often he circled around deeper gullies, and avoided patches of tall grass or timber.

Toward evening, they had not made much progress. Drom chafed at the delay, but he understood it. The dwarf was young, but he knew this land and his caution was exemplary.

Even so, it was not enough. As the long shadows of dusk spread slowly over the land, making it more beautiful than it was, there was a loud cry from a ridge only several hundred feet away.

Drom snapped his head up at the noise He saw a lone goblin, arms waving.

"Hurry!" commanded Kentanos. "Where there is one, there are likely others."

They broke into a gallop. Down into a gulley they went, and the dwarf, barely puffing, jogged along with them. When they came out, and rode up to somewhat higher ground, Drom looked back.

The lone elug was gone. He was now just one of many, for a troop of a dozen goblins stood where he had done.

They did not stand long. Even as Drom watched they raced forward, swords drawn and harsh battle cries filling the air. The noise was distant, but audible.

Down the travelers descended into another gully. Water splashed up at the horses hooves, and the dwarf struggled a little with his heavy boots. Then he led them at a zigzag up the side of the gully and into another.

They could not see the pursuing goblins. For several moments, they could not hear them. Then the battle cries were loud again as the troop climbed higher ground.

Night was drawing on. "Will the dark help us?" Drom yelled to the dwarf as they sped forward.

Kentanos gave a single shake of his head as he ran close by.

"No! Goblins see better in the dark than even dwarves. We will be at a disadvantage."

It was bad news, but not unexpected. The goblins lived underground, and stories credited them with the ability to see in the dark.

It seemed to Drom the best chance was to outpace their foes, yet the terrain was not good for fast galloping, and the goblins, sensing an enemy close by, hastened at an alarming pace. He was not sure if they could keep that up, but legend once again indicated they could.

With a leap Kentanos cleared an ancient log, half rotted and covered in fungi. It was one of the few in the area. The horses followed, and immediately the dwarf turned northward and upslope.

It was the wrong direction. The travelers needed to get out of this accursed land of devastating magics and goblins, but the korrig warrior led the way as though he knew exactly what he was doing. And more importantly, where he was going.

They ran downhill soon after, and found themselves in a dried up watercourse. Rocks and pebbles lined it, and it was dangerous for though the surface was dry, in those places where there was sand both dwarf and horses sunk into it.

Suddenly the dwarf veered to the side. Nothing was different here save a large boulder, and certainly there was no path. Not that Drom could see.

Yet straight as an arrow Kentanos climbed the bank, and the horses followed. It was hard going. Rocks and pebbles dislodged beneath them, sliding down to the bottom. The earth itself seemed to seethe and move, but they made it to the top.

At that high point Cadawn wheeled his horse around and looked behind them. The goblins had gained.

"We must stop and fight!" he called.

Kentanos kept running. "No! Follow me!"

The others paused. No word they spoke, but they each felt doubt. It was Drom who broke the indecision.

He kicked his mount forward and it shot off after Kentanos. The others followed. Cadawn was their leader, yet Drom trusted in the dwarf. As a people, he liked them all. Yet there was something about the youngster who reminded him of himself, and if you asked for a guide it was best to follow them in their own land.

They climbed higher. The shouts of the goblins were loud now, interspersed with battle cries, taunts and insults. The land was barren again, completely devoid of any life. Even the sand and rock were black, as though once the very stone in this place had burned.

Kentanos headed for the highest ground. They followed a ridge, and soon would come to the end of it. At that point the hill crested, yet a strange rock formation pierced the sky like a tall chimney.

"Quickly!" the korrig warrior called. He had been true to his word about keeping up with the horses. For the most part, he even outpaced them. He could not have done so on flat ground, but in this landscape two legs and a shorter stride were an advantage.

They came to the top. The goblins pursuing had gained yet again, and the clamor of their approach was hideous. There would be no prisoner-taking here by surprise. There would only be battle and death.

The travelers were at the crest of the hill, and they were trapped. The other side fell in a wildly steep slope of scree, impossible to ride over. Behind them the goblins were already making the same ascent the travelers had just clambered themselves.

Drom dismounted, sword in hand. This was no place to ride in battle. He would stand his ground and sell his life in blood protecting Ariane until the last.

The goblins came on. There was a burst of sound, thunderous yet hollow, and Drom swung around. Kentanos was heaving against a stone door at the base of the chimney-like structure. Where once seemed solid stone, now a gap appeared, growing wider.

Cadawn flung his weight behind the stone door to help, and it slid open. It was dark as the pit inside, and the horses balked. There was no chance of getting them to go in.

"Quickly!" Cadawn said. "Get what supplies you can and scare the horses off!"

This they did, and sent them galloping away.

"My people will find and care for them, with luck," the dwarf said. "Now inside. Fast!"

A light sprang up from the inner floor with a wave of the druid's hand. Then they were through the doorway and Kentanos and Drom pushed the stone shut again. When it was closed, the dwarf secured it with iron bolts.

From outside came the faintest whisper of screams and curses, then louder the smashing of rocks and stones. The door did not move, yet still Kentanos shook his head.

"That is a secret door rather than a fortress door. Now that it's discovered, the goblins will break through, even if it takes them some time."

"We need a little rest," Cadawn said. "We don't have the endurance of dwarves."

They rested momentarily, and Drom caught his breath. It was disconcerting to hear the clamor from outside. The goblins had found larger stones, the size of a person perhaps, and these they must have been heaving at the door, even if it took a half dozen of them to shift the weight. So it seemed from the booming noises, and the fine dust that filtered down from the ceiling at each strike.

"We must go!" Kentanos said "It isn't safe for us here."

20. Goblin Tracks

The dwarf led them forward. From a stone shelf near the door he had procured one of the strange lanterns Gorik's band had used on attacking the goblins. Its light was strong, and Cadawn let his enchantment that had served as illumination until then fade.

"Gorik feared this," the young dwarf said. He glanced at the travelers as they hurried forward. "The goblins stir, and he did not think we would reach the borders of the realm without more trouble. So, for my safety, and for yours, he instructed me to break, if necessary, a command of the king that no outsider ever be shown our secret ways underground."

"He won't be punished for helping us?" Arian asked.

Kentanos kept going at a fast pace, and his answer was breathy.

"Some fast talking will be needed, but between the news you have brought, and that a druid is with you, he thought the king would understand and approve his judgement. It's a stern rule, yet all rules must be broken at need."

More dust came from above, and this time there was a plod of several pebbles.

"Hurry!" Kentanos commanded.

Drom was not sure what the urgency was, but the korrig warrior certainly feared something. They hurried after him while he strode at a great pace despite his shortness.

Soon they came to a round chamber, and the dwarf stopped.

"We're here," he said.

"Where?" Drom asked.

"To a place of safety. Give me a hand, when I'm ready."

Kentanos passed his hand over the wall to the left, and found what he was looking for. There was a click, and another secret door opened. It was not meant to walk through, being only a foot high and several feet long, but the stone pivoted out to reveal a heavy chain. The rings were as thick as a man's finger.

The dwarf pulled the chain out until a length of it ran over the ground. Then he did the same on the other side.

"What's this?" Drom asked.

"I think I understand," Cadawn said. "The dwarves are famous for tunneling and clever contraptions. When the chains are pulled, they'll trigger a mechanism and collapse the roof of the tunnel we just came through."

Kentanos grinned, and in the light of the lantern it looked wicked.

"Exactly. The entrance outside is revealed to the goblins now. It's useless to the dwarves, and if the goblins don't break through and come down now, they will some other time. Most of our secret doors are protected, one way or another."

The dwarf took hold of the chain on the right side. He signaled then to Drom.

"Pull the one on the left exactly when I say," he instructed. "The mechanism should work with one chain alone, but two will make it certain."

Drom lifted the chain. The metal was cold in his hands, and heavy. He inched back until it drew somewhat taught, just as Kentanos was doing.

The dwarf glanced at him. "Ready?" he asked.

"When you give the word," Drom said.

"On the count of one," Kentanos replied. "Three. Two. One!"

Drom heaved at the chain. He did not know what it was connected to, but it required no great effort. He felt something give on the other end, deep in the stone, and then the chain went slack again. No wonder Kentanos had been nervous coming down the tunnel. The trap that was set required barely any force to trigger, or perhaps the chains were rigged in such a way that their weight did most of the work once they were set in motion.

"Back now!" cried the dwarf. "Back and down!"

Kentanos wasted no time. He picked up his lantern that he had set on the floor and ran a dozen paces to an arched doorway ahead. The rest followed him. Straight ahead the tunnel went, but there was an alcove to the left. The dwarf dived into it, rolling to the ground.

"Down!" he yelled.

They followed him, and Drom covered Ariane with his body.

A moment of silence followed, heavy with expectation. Strangely, what followed was the sound of swift-running water muffled by stone. When it was gone, the silence was profound.

It did not last long. The very earth itself muttered as stone moved and the weight of the hillside shifted. Then there was a groan and a mighty crash that seemed so loud as to hurt the ears.

Following fast after was a gust of wind stronger than a tempest. It howled down the corridor, and dust and debris blew with it.

Drom could barely breathe. He wrapped his cloak about his face and saw dimly the others doing the same. For a long while they coughed and sneezed, while the earth grew quiet once more around them.

151

The dwarf was the first to stand up, and the others followed. The air was still heavy with dust, and the light of the lantern lit each particle up like a brown mist.

"That was a beauty!" Kentanos said with enthusiasm. "Come look at this."

They followed him out of the alcove. The tunnel down which they had come to enter the round chamber was gone. No goblins would be following them. Out into the round chamber itself a mass of earth and rocks had issued, half filling it.

"Well," said Cadawn, "the famed skill of the dwarves is clear to see. Just as well for us that we have you for a guide."

Kentanos bowed, a smile still on his face. "The guiding is not done yet. Nor are we out of danger. We have merely exchanged one problem for another, but with luck we'll win through to the end without further event."

The smile was gone by the time he finished speaking. Drom liked that he rejoiced in the skill of his people, but clearly there were dangers underground.

"Let me guess," he said. "There are goblins in these tunnels too?"

"I'll explain as we walk," the dwarf suggested. "Better to get out of this dust. It'll linger in the air a long time."

He led them down the tunnel. Soon it came to a crossroads, and he veered right.

"This is all korrig work," Kentanos said. "The earth under most of the Broken Lands is delved. Either by us or the goblins. The tunneling has been going on since before the elù-haraken. Where we are now is safe. It's known only to us, unless the goblins have discovered it recently. That's always a chance. It does not take us where you need to go though."

Drom was not liking the direction this was going. "So how do we do that, then?"

"Well, there are many, many tunnels. Some are controlled by us, and some by the goblins, irrespective of who delved them first. The war goes on underground at least as much as it does above."

They came to a ramp, sloping down, with an opening to the left that seemed level. Kentanos led them downward without hesitation.

"We each have tunnels that have not been discovered, such as this. But most of the delving is a no-man's-land, where dwarf and goblin both stalk in the shadows at their peril."

Drom was beginning to understand. "So for us to go in the direction we need, we must enter that no-man's-land?"

"That we must do."

Ariane's eyes gleamed in the semi-dark as Drom looked at her, but there was no fear in them.

They went forward, but Kentanos took his time now. Drom understood. The last information the dwarves had was that this area of the delving had not been discovered by the goblins, but that was always subject to change at any time. He went forward cautiously himself, his hand ready to draw his sword at an instant.

By what power the lantern operated, Drom did not know. He never saw the dwarf fill it with any kind of oil. It just burned with a steady light, and kept on burning.

Even so, Kentanos manipulated shutters on the lamp to reduce the light. Their eyes were growing more accustomed to the dark anyway, but mostly it must be to make the travelers less easy to spot themselves should goblins be nearby.

Drom had no idea of the time, but Kentanos called a halt some while later.

"It's two hours before midnight," he said. "Time for us to rest and sleep."

153

There was, of course, no chance for a fire. There was no timber. About them the walls had drawn in close. This was no longer delving, but a natural cave system.

They rested in a little nook in the wall. The ceiling was low above them, and before and behind there was gravel. Should anything approach in the dark, they would hear it.

A watch was still kept. Drom took his turn, and then slept peacefully. He did not like it underground, but it did not worry him. In that he was similar to Kentanos. Yet the druid and Ariane were anxious, even if they tried to hide it.

There was no morning. In the deep dark, the lantern Kentanos carried suddenly shone.

"The sun is up outside," the korrig warrior said. "With luck, before it sets, we'll be above ground again and close to the outer border of the korrig realm."

They ate a hasty breakfast. Whatever the danger, they were all ready to face it if it meant getting to the outside world again.

It was silent in the dark caves. All sign of delving was now gone, and they passed through an underground realm that nature had made. Some caverns were vast. In other places they crawled on hands and knees with a rough roof scraping their backs.

At times there were underground pools with strange, white fish. Sometimes there was the sound of rushing water. It came to them dimly through walls of stone.

Kentanos grinned at them at one such place. "The korrig know where to delve and where to leave alone. A single blow of hammer and chisel in some caves can unleash a flood. In others, it can topple a hill. Best to walk carefully."

The dwarf carried on, whistling softly at times while he walked.

After their midday meal though he stopped whistling, and he went forward carefully.

"We are close now to new tunnels. Be wary. Goblins have not been this way in years, but they know the place where I'll now lead you."

Nothing much seemed to change except that they walked uphill now. At times the way was steep, and there was loose rock underfoot that made walking quietly nearly impossible. The dwarf managed it though, even in his heavy boots.

There was a drip of water, and the walls were slick with moisture at times. Kentanos paused at one such place, studying it closely.

"Just a few more paces, I think," he said.

Drom was sure the dwarves had a way of leaving secret markings. If what they had traveled was just a tiny amount of the delvings beneath the earth, then no one could remember all the different routes. There would be marks, signposts of a kind, but they would be secret.

He did not ask Kentanos. The dwarf would not tell him. Such knowledge was the difference between life and death, and should the goblins discover it things would go badly for the dwarves.

Kentanos paused near the wall. He glanced at it keenly for a while, and then placed his head against the stone for a long time.

"I hear nothing on the other side," he said. "But be ready, and be quiet."

Drom drew his sword. It gleamed dully in the lantern light, but as always it felt good and a rush of excitement swept through him. He wished for no goblins to be on the other side, but if there were some, they would die swiftly.

His heart thumped, and impatience filled him. Maybe he wanted a fight, after all. It was what he was born for, and if there were no cheering fans to encourage him, he could hear the memory of them in his mind regardless.

What Kentanos did, Drom did not see. Yet suddenly the wall pivoted. A door swung open, and for all the weight of it, it made less than a whisper of sound.

The dwarf went through, lantern in one hand and axe in the other. Drom followed swiftly. It was with regret that he saw no one and nothing. It was just another corridor.

He realized he was slipping back into the temperament of the arena, and a chill went through him. He knew that side of himself, and he did not like it. He had forced it down for two decades, but fighting once more had brought it to the surface.

The others came through. Kentanos hushed them, and then listened once more.

"I hear nothing," he said. "We must take great care though. We're not safe here."

He closed the door. It slid without noise and when it was still Drom could see no sign at all of its presence. It looked just the same as the rest of the wall.

Kentanos grinned at him. "It's good dwarf work. You'll not see it's like again, I'll wager."

The dwarf led them off again, but he did so slowly. The lantern was shuttered even more, and only a sliver of light escaped. It was just enough to see by, and no more.

Kentanos studied the ground as they went. His back was bent a little, and his head was down. He paused at one point, only a dozen or so paces from the door, then went on.

After a dozen more paces he stopped again. This time he took his time, and then whispered to them in solemn tones.

"Goblin tracks," he said. "Fresh in the dust, but I can't say how many. Quite a few by the looks of it. Be ready for an attack at any moment."

Drom gripped tight the hilt of his sword. They were not alone down here, but he did not really mind. The thrill of anticipation ran through him.

21. The Rumor of War

Kentanos extinguished his lamp. It was pitch dark beneath the earth, and they could see nothing.

Yet their sight adjusted after a little while, so that when the dwarf unshuttered his lamp by the barest margin, they could see.

"More light than that," Kentanos told them, "is to risk being seen by goblins long before we have at least the chance to see or hear them."

He led them forward, and he did so with great care. Often he would pause and listen, before moving on at a slow pace.

They had hoped to be above ground by sunset, but they all knew that was not possible now. They were going far too slowly, but there was no help for it.

In the distance they heard faint noises and the dwarf paused.

"Drums," he whispered, and went on.

Drom could barely hear it. Yet not long after they climbed a set of rough-hewn stairs and turned left at the top. Soon they came to a crossroads, and suddenly the noises were louder.

Boom. Boom. Bam. Bam. Boom.

It was an unnerving beat, and it throbbed through the darkness with menace. They were underground, right in the heart of territory, for now at least, frequented by goblins. If they were discovered, their fate was certain.

Even so, the dwarf led them forward with a confident, if slow step. Drom soon understood why.

Clearly some sort of goblin ceremony was going on. That would distract them. Better still, who would expect a small party of enemies to walk among them?

The best place to hide was in plain sight. Drom had learned that long ago. Down here the tunnel systems were vast, and the chances of being seen by a goblin remote. The enemy would be watching the entrances to this place, or at least those they knew of, and that was all.

He was proved wrong though, almost immediately. His first warning was the complete shuttering of the lamp. The dark descended once more, and the crash of the drums throbbed through the air.

In the blackness they waited, and Kentanos obviously dared not even whisper a warning. They all knew what his cutting out of the light must mean though.

Within moments a pinprick of light appeared ahead of them, then the slapping of bare feet on the stone floor. Shadowy figures appeared, vague and obscure, but coming closer.

The travelers pressed themselves against the wall, and Drom, sword drawn, placed the blade behind his leg so it would not glint.

It was a tense moment. Yet as swift as the danger appeared, it disappeared also. The bobbing light turned right and vanished. There was a crossroads ahead, and the goblins had taken a different route.

No one moved for some time, then Kentanos let loose the smallest sliver of light. They followed him to the crossroads. Of the goblins, they could neither hear nor see anything.

"We must go ahead," the korrig warrior whispered. "There is no other way. Not unless you forgo your destination and return with me to the dwarven halls."

That was not a possibility. Not for them, and the dwarf did not expect anyone to change their mind. After a moment, he went ahead.

Without doubt, Kentanos was risking his life for the travelers. Drom knew it, and he admired him for it. This was a mission he had volunteered for, and he had known when he did so it would be dangerous. That took either courage or stupidity. And the dwarf, if young, was not stupid.

Boom. Boom. Bam. Bam. Boom, beat the drums of the goblins, seemingly close at times and at others farther away. Yet now they heard fell voices in the air, screaming and crying out in some rite of their dark kind that no human had likely seen before. It grated on Drom's mind, for there was evil in the shadows and though he could interpret no words he sensed the darkness of the rite.

At times they saw the ruddy glow of burning torches in the distance, and once they had to backtrack and hide down a side tunnel as a large group of goblins passed by closely. Even when they were gone, the reek of smoke remained in the air, and fear with it. The underground halls seemed alive with the enemy.

"Where are these groups going to?" Drom whispered when they set forth again.

"Nowhere," the korrig warrior answered. "I think these are patrols. The goblins guess we are here, or fear it. They should all be at their rite, yet many wander the corridors, searching…"

It was hard to tell the time in the dark. It felt like they had been down here for weeks, and certainly progress was far slower than they had expected. Then, once again, they saw a pinprick of light ahead.

They moved backward in the dark, shuffling as quietly as they could some twenty paces or so. There was a crossroads there, and even as the light grew steadily brighter as goblins advanced, they took the left corridor and waited.

The goblins came to the crossroad, and there they spoke in guttural tones. There were at least six of them so far as Drom could tell.

"...orders have been given," snarled one.

"Always orders! Do this! Do that! Go there! Come back again!" answered another. The words came out as though he chewed on gravel and spat it out.

"What?" said the first. "Is that the usual whining and whinging you little folk give? Or is it disobedience?"

There was a silence, and the first goblin seemed to swell up in size. Drom could see him dimly, for the light of the goblin that held the torch was on the other side of him.

"Little folk obey. That's what we do, isn't it? Always."

"So it should be. When I say we patrol, we patrol. If you can't do this, what good will you be in the war?"

"We can kill. Yes we can. We can kill nicely," said the other. "We already kill the stinking korrig." He spat when he finished.

"Not like this. That's just for fun. What's coming soon is big, I tell you. Big. Better be ready for it. Now come along. When we're done we can go back to the party. Maybe the feasting will be about to start then."

To Drom's dismay the group started moving again, and the torch flared and bobbed, growing closer. The travelers' luck had run out, and the goblins were coming straight toward them.

Dismay turned to anticipation. Drom felt the hilt of the sword in his hand, and the lust for battle rose up in him once more. He knew it better than an old friend, and he could barely hold himself still.

Yet still he remained, and his companions. Every second brought the enemy closer, but when the trap sprung it would be quicker for it.

The goblins were close when they suddenly halted, and one of them hissed.

Boom. Boom. Bam. Bam. Boom.

Drom leaped from the shadows of the wall. His sword arced, the blade ruddy in the torchlight, and killed. A head toppled with a thud to the stone floor.

Kentanos was silent. No battle cry of the dwarves escaped his lips. Yet his axe whistled and it crumpled ribs and spilled intestines.

This was a fight that must be finished quickly, before an alarm could be raised. And none of the goblins could be allowed to escape lest a thousand of them were alarmed and took up pursuit of the enemy in their midst.

Drom swung around to face another, and steel clattered as sword struck sword. Showers of sparks ignited as the blades screeched together in furious combat. It was no battle of skill against skill but shear desperation to live. Yet ere the sparks faded another goblin lay dead.

Leaping closer to the dwarf, Drom saw that he had killed another goblin and even as he watched the axe dispatched one more.

Only one was left. It was the leader, taller and thicker set than the others. His eyes, red rimmed and ferocious, gleamed with hatred, then with a scream he ran back toward the crossroads.

"Down!" cried the druid. "Down!"

Drom dropped to the floor. The dwarf was near him, panting, axe in his hands and gore running from the blade onto the floor.

The goblin screamed again, loud and piercing. It was not fright, or at least not only that. It was a call to his brethren.

162

Light flashed, brilliant against the dark. It was silver-white, tinged with blue at the edges. As lightning it flew, hissing through the air, and the goblin was, for a hundredth part of a heartbeat, outlined with incredible clarity against the shadows ahead.

Then the goblin burst into flame and disappeared in a vortex of writhing arms, legs and red tongues of devouring magic.

Boom. Boom. Bam. Bam. Boom! Went the drums, and then a profound silence descended.

Kentanos was the first to move. "Quickly! Take their clothes. That scream will have been heard. We must look as the enemy if we're a chance to get out of here."

They did as instructed. The clothes stank of body odor, and were covered in filth. Yet there were dark cloaks, and these they took and wrapped around themselves. The curved swords they took also, even Ariane, and they did not sheathe them. They must look the part of marauding goblins, bent on finding intruders.

The torch was still burning on the floor, and Kentanos picked it up. He looked just like a goblin in its ruddy glow. They left the bodies behind them, and came to what was left of the one Cadawn had killed.

"Strange," the dwarf said. "he was a hobgoblin. A different breed of elug if you will, and not normally seen in these parts. He is down from the mountains. More news I must take to the king. And most of all that a great war is brewing. Swiftly now! Follow my lead if we encounter more of the enemy!"

They did not walk any more. Kentanos led them at a jog. The faster they were away from the bodies the better it would be for them.

It was mostly silent in the dark halls, and the drums had ceased. Yet there were fell voices in the air, at times close by and at others faint. There were corridors everywhere,

163

breaking off left and right repeatedly, and rooms with stone doors, often open.

22. I Go No Farther

It was mayhem in the dark corridors. Shouts broke out everywhere, and often the travelers saw torches ahead and took a side tunnel to avoid them.

Kentanos led them without hesitation. He must have been through here at another time when goblins did not occupy it, or else he followed some logic to the maze of caverns that only a dwarf could understand. Whatever the situation, he led them unerringly and with confidence, and always he got them on a path that led upwards again.

Surely there was an exit somewhere near. Drom was torn between the lust to fight and the desire to get out from this dreary labyrinth beneath the earth where danger lurked around every bend.

Without warning they took a right turn at a crossroads and found a troop of goblins marching straight at them, their own torch spluttering and reeking of smoke.

Kentanos was in the lead. He looked like a goblin, if no one looked too closely. Drom knew he was himself too large, but he might pass for a hobgoblin. Ariane was shorter, and her beauty was hidden by the dirty rags of the slain goblin she wore. Cadawn was tall though, far too tall for a goblin. Yet even as Drom glanced at him he saw that the druid was bent down, and the flickering light seemed strange around him, deepening the shadows. It was good fortune, or perhaps a touch of druid magic.

Unexpectedly the dwarf cried out. "*Hrakash.*" Then again, even louder, "hrakash!"

The two parties suddenly stopped. The dwarf pointed behind him with his bent sword and cried out again.

"They come!"

Drom had never heard the word hrakash. He guessed it was something the goblins understood though. Some of them fled, and the remainder stood in doubt.

Kentanos ran, bumping into a goblin but not attacking it, and something about his manner inspired fear. The remaining goblins ran back the way they had come, those they sought running undetected with them.

Drom slowed down when they came to a crossroad. His companions did the same, and while the goblins disappeared into the gloom ahead the travelers took the left path and started to run again.

Soon they came to a set of stairs, ascended it, and then turned right at another crossroad. There the dwarf stopped, and he listened.

"Nothing," he said after a moment. "They've not realized."

Cadawn laughed quietly in the shadows.

"A good trick," he said.

"What trick?" Ariane asked. "The strange word?"

"Strange indeed," the druid replied. "Goblins largely speak a mixture of older and new versions of our own tongue. They learned this during the Shadowed Wars when many different tribes fought together, each with their own language. They could not talk among each other, so they took up the speech of evil men who often served as their captains. They still have their own languages though. Mostly just a few words are left, and hrakash is one likely understood by all the tribes."

"What does it mean?"

"Elf!" the dwarf answered. "Of old goblins and elves were bitter enemies, and no people scare them as much. Not even the dwarves, though we come close."

166

They moved on after that, and quickly. At times they still heard shouts and calls, and twice more they saw distant lights, but they met no more goblins.

Up they went, and the passageways became somewhat grand.

"Korrig stone work," the dwarf said. "Good quality, too. Alas, for our people were in the past far more numerous than now."

Three flights of stairs they ascended, and the last had a marble balustrade, carved with vines and flowers. Then Kentanos paused at a fork in the road. One went straight ahead, and it was broad and even. The other angled upward, and was narrow and rough.

"Straight ahead is the main way," the dwarf said. "It's the quickest way out, but though we haven't seen any goblins for a while, the door at the end is likely guarded. They'll have discovered it, certainly."

"And the other path?" Cadawn asked.

"There's a door there too, but the way is longer and rougher. But that door is well concealed, and there's no reason for goblins to be there. Of course, there might be enemies somewhere along that path too."

"The safer way, I suggest," Cadawn said. "We don't need any more fighting if we can avoid it."

The dwarf nodded in agreement. "It's the best way for us, but be careful. There are ways to die up there that don't need the presence of goblins."

He led them onward, and they swiftly saw what he meant. Mostly, the way forward was no longer carved tunnels but a natural cave system. The floor was uneven, often just loose stones that rattled and shifted beneath their boots.

Moisture ran down the walls in places, and at others they crossed ponds of cold water, still as a mirror but dark.

Kentanos began to use his lantern again, and discarded the torch. It was nearly burned out.

There were times when they were forced to crawl on hands and knees, and then even to wriggle on their stomachs. Yet the way was never completely closed and they came to wider caverns.

There were bats, and they took to flight in a flurry of dark wings when they were disturbed, and the smell of their excrement was strong.

"Forward!" said the dwarf. "We're close now."

He was right. They ascended a steep tunnel, the floor of which moved beneath them. Rocks gave way. Excrement was thick, and filled with maggots. Yet they clambered to the top, not without some cursing. Mostly from Drom.

Ariane glanced at him reproachfully, her face white as chalk in the dim light. Drom swore all the more, and put his heart into it.

They came to the top of the slope, and a narrow tunnel branched to the right. Drom did not think a person could fit through it. To the left was another tunnel. It looked the same to Drom, but Kentanos wriggled through without hesitation.

The rest of them followed, and in just moments came to a cave. It was larger, though not large. The floor was stone, covered in dust, and the korrig warrior inspected it.

"Elugs have been here," he said, "but found nothing. Their skill is not as the korrig's."

He immediately went to the left side of the cave. The wall was sheer there, yet a pile of broken rubble from it allowed him to climb up near the roof. There, as he often did, he listened.

Evidently he heard nothing he did not expect. He ran his hands over the surface, and once more a dwarven door twisted open.

It seemed just as dark outside as within. Yet Kentanos shuttered his lantern, and went through.

Quickly, the others followed. Drom came last, and he nearly cried when he felt the sweet air of night on his face and breathed it in like wine.

The night was fading around them. Dawn had come, gray, and even in this desolate land, beautiful. The dry waste was made fair. The harsh ridges of stone, jagged and chaotic, now spoke of order and symmetry. The cry of birds to greet the sun was as music, and the sweet air was life.

"We made it," Ariane said. "Aroth is with us. Can you not feel his presence?"

Drom was not sure of that. He felt as though a shadow had been lifted from him though. In the caverns, his old self had woken. He had wanted to fight, and to spill blood. It was a side to his mind that he had long detested, and long striven to shed like a snake its skin. Yet it would always be with him.

Outside though, and free, he knew he could be more than a gladiator. He was silent as the rim of the sun showed itself, climbing out of the sea of night and banishing darkness.

Kentanos pointed. "See there? The sun lights it up for us, and shows you your way. That is Brandwil Fortress."

Drom looked, and saw. It was distant, but probably less than a day's march. On a hill, green now in the sun and beyond the Broken Lands, was a huge construct of stone. Almost it looked like yet another ridge, but it was larger than most, and the straight lines of laid stone were clear to see as were the towers and turrets and fortress walls.

"Nearly there," Cadawn said. "Soon we'll walk where one of the great of Alithoras held court. There he ruled and gave judgements. There he formed an army to withstand the might of the Dark, for a time. There hope

169

was born, and the promise of a better future. All dust now. Buried beneath a sea of evil. Yet once it was the beating heart of Camlanta, and the Light he created yet endures, even if only in dim legend. If it can be remembered though, it can be rekindled."

Strange words, thought Drom. The druid had caught something of the mood of Ariane.

The dwarf closed the door behind them. Once more it seemed as though nothing had ever been there save the natural stone. The legends about dwarves spoke truly concerning their skill as craftsmen. Likewise, so far as Drom could see, about everything else.

Kentanos took them down the slope, and away from the door he thought the goblins would be guarding. They rested for some two hours of the morning in a rocky dell that should hide them from any prying eyes.

Cadawn kept watch while the others slept. It seemed that he needed no rest, but Drom suspected otherwise. He used magic to sustain himself while the others who could not rested as they must.

It was still midmorning when they woke, a little refreshed but still in need of more rest. Yet they feared the goblins would find them, and the further away they were by nightfall the better.

"This is where we part," Kentanos told them. "The korrig realm ends here. And I can go no more with you."

"Will you be safe?" Ariane asked.

"Safe or not, I must try to warn my people of the coming war. Fear not though. There is a korrig stronghold nearby, and there I'll get help."

"Farewell then," Cadawn said. "Darkness is spreading over the land as evil wakes. Your people will not be the only ones in peril. All over Camlanta trouble will be brewing. It's our part, if we succeed, to stop that. Your help has been vital, and we thank you. Long live the korrig!"

The dwarf trudged off soon after, clambering over the countryside with determination and purpose. Once more the travelers were by themselves, and Cadawn led them as he had before.

They headed toward the fortress, which grew in size swiftly as they marched.

23. The Ruins of Glory

The travelers passed over the land from noon to dusk like ghosts. Cadawn led them, and there was clear determination in his every glance and a sense of purpose to his every stride. He was approaching the end of his quest, and he would not risk it by being seen.

Drom kept a lookout, sharper than even normal. It was his fault they had been captured the first time, though it was dark and the goblins could see better than him. Even so, it was still his fault, and he would not let it happen again if he could help it.

The land was empty though. Not only did they see no sign of goblins, but there was no living thing at all. It was a brooding silence, as though a malevolent being walked it with them, scaring all life away.

If Cadawn sensed something untoward, he made no comment. Nor did Ariane, yet often her gaze searched the waste around them. Perhaps she looked for goblins. Or maybe something else.

They spoke little. It was hard going on foot, and Drom missed the horses. The thought of them being captured by goblins made his blood boil, but he did not think they would have been. He believed they would be found and cared for by the dwarves. They did not ride, but they had a reputation for kindness to animals. And strangers.

All around them the land began to change, and swiftly. It was as though they passed some unseen barrier. Behind them was barren waste. Almost within the space of a few hundred feet the grass sprang up, green and lush. Trees grew, oaks especially, and flowering bushes favored the higher trail they followed.

It was still silent though.

They trudged on, and Brandwil Fortress loomed large before them. The shadows of afternoon swept over it, hiding the degradation of time. The broken towers did not stand out so much. The minarets seemed majestic, piercing the sky. The battered walls took on an even, dark tone.

The fortress brooded like the land. It hulked against the sky, massive and impregnable. Yet Brandwil had been killed inside it, though the stories were vague. The fortress had not saved him, yet it was not said that he lost either.

Night fell. "I think we're safe from the goblins now," Cadawn said. "Reasonably so, anyway. Yet there may be other dangers beside them. I think we should camp for the night, and explore the fortress in the light of day."

Ariane agreed. "I feel the history of this place," she said. "The good and the bad. The land remembers still, but there is a darkness here too. I know not if it belongs here, or it comes with us. Regardless, we must be on guard."

They set up camp in a grove of oaks. It was little more than a score of trees, but they seemed tall and healthy. There was no real running water, but a spring trickled from the base of a large rock. There was water there, if they were patient, to serve their needs.

Drom liked their camp. There were fallen branches everywhere, and no one could enter the grove without making noise. He agreed with Cadawn that the goblins were no longer a threat. They were busy preparing for war against the dwarves, but that did not mean a party of them might not follow the traveler's tracks, if they could see them in the dark. Or, as the stories sometimes said, scent them.

173

The next morning, under a bright sun, they climbed the ancient road that led to the fortress.

"The staff I seek may not be here," Cadawn said. "But I think we're close. Certainly we must explore this place. Who knows what we may learn? And if the staff isn't here, we may still find a clue."

At the top of the road they came to the gate of the fortress. The guard towers had partly crumbled, and they picked their way through rubble. The gate itself stood open. It was a twisted thing of rusted iron. Time had eaten away at it. An enemy had battered it. Fire or magic had blasted it. Yet still it was mostly intact. It was the massive hinges that had given way.

Slowly, they walked inside. It felt to Drom like stepping into a legend. Through these very gates Brandwil himself had ridden, and his knights and armies with him. The stonework was coming apart, and weeds twisted their way through broken flagstones. Even so, Brandwil would have known every stone and would recognize this place a thousand years after. Nothing had really changed that greatly.

Their footsteps echoed in the killing ground between the two towers. Slits in the walls provided space for arrows to be shot. Gaps in the ceiling allowed for boiling water or oil to be poured.

It was not a pleasant place to walk. The shadows gathered deeply about them and studied these intruders who broke their restful silence.

How long since living people had come here? Drom could not guess. No doubt travelers had passed through from time to time. It could easily be a hundred years since the last though.

They came out the other side of the tunnel. There was a set of ruined gates there too. Beyond, a vast courtyard opened up.

Cadawn sighed. "Here, in this very place, the fabled knights of Camlanta gathered to ride out to war or quests. Think of it! The walls around us would have echoed with the clatter of hooves. This was the heart of all that was good. For a time."

"Even gods die," Ariane answered. "Nothing lasts forever."

"Yes, but gods can be resurrected. At least so we hope. And maybe more."

Drom was not sure what the druid was saying. It seemed as though he foresaw a time when the Light ruled in the realm once again, and an age of chivalry and nobility returned. It would be a drastic change from the present where the populace watched men kill each other in the arena for entertainment. And the king's will was law, unchecked by custom or balancing authority.

They explored the fortress, and it was vast. Much was still in good repair. They climbed stairs and walked parapets that remained serviceable. Others they avoided for the stones had collapsed into rubble, or looked like they soon might.

They found nothing though. Nothing save the remnants of a time that was, devoid of life the same as a person who had ceased to breathe. The body was there that once housed the spirit, but it was empty like an abandoned home.

They left the keep to the last. It was the final refuge of a fortress. It was the last defense against attack. Now, it was the last place to search for the staff, or some clue as to its hiding place.

Drom did not think it was here. He did not really understand the purposes of the druid of old called Conhain. He knew the hearts of men though. A talisman of hope for the future would not be hidden in what was, essentially, a tomb.

The more he thought of it that way, the more he believed he was right. The fortress was a grave marker for a time that had passed. He did not think it would return regardless of what Conhain hinted at.

They ascended the central staircase of the keep. There were many rooms, and levels, and the wooden floors were mostly intact. Some showed signs of scorch marks though. Again, it might be fire or magic. Either way the flames had been subdued before they caught too much.

"This was the last area of fighting, according to the druid histories," Cadawn said. "Brandwil retreated to the top, and we're nearly there."

"Retreated from whom?" Ariane asked.

Drom was not sure of the answer himself and wanted to know. He had heard many stories of Brandwil's last fight, and none of them were the same.

"Not the Dark," Cadawn said. "Not goblins or dragons or trolls. It was civil war. He left his realm in the hands of his nephew while he helped the elves to the east. When he returned, he found his cousin had usurped the throne, held his wife as hostage, and the fortress against him."

"So it was Brandwil himself who fought his way into his own fortress?" Drom could hardly believe it.

"So it was. With his druid and his army."

They came to the final floor of the keep. "It was in this very place, with most of their armies dead, that Brandwil and his nephew fought in single combat. Sword to sword, and sword to spear when the nephew's blade broke. Here the traitor was killed, and the victory went to Brandwil. Yet what victory could there be when his people had been divided by treachery and most slain in civil war?"

"Brandwil lived then?" Ariane asked.

"Ah, that is a good question. Even the druid histories are vague on that point. It seems no one really knew, and Brandwil's druid was killed, or disappeared as well.

Whatever the truth, the tradition among the druids of Car Sagoth was that Brandwil was gravely injured. Maybe even mortally injured. Some say that he was buried nearby. Others under a mountain or a river, whose course was diverted and then returned to hide him. But in all cases, he was taken from here by three creatures of faery, and never seen again."

"Nor will be," Drom said, "until the hour of Camlanta's greatest need."

"Yes. That's the story, and the druid tradition also."

They searched this last place of fighting, but there was nothing left. Over the centuries, the fortress would have been despoiled of anything of value.

"That's it then?" Drom said.

"Not quite," the druid replied.

"The druid records say there's a trapdoor to a turret at the very top." He pointed at the central area of the ceiling, distinguished by a carved wooden knob. "Right there, I think."

It looked to Drom as though it was nothing but an ornament on a ceiling and walls that had many, such as carved architraves and multicolored panels. Yet, especially after his experience with Kentanos, he was willing to admit that secret doors could be hidden anywhere.

They gathered rubble from a corner of the room where a pillar had toppled, and with it they created a platform on which to stand.

Cadawn stood upon it, and reached the knob. He turned it and pulled on it to no effect, yet when he pressed upward against it there was a click and faint cracks appeared in a square shape. Daylight leaked through them.

The druid pushed the door up on its hinges, rusty and squeaky, and climbed up. Drom and Ariane went next.

At the top was a simple turret, walled to waist high but with no roof. It was exposed to the air and rain, and there was nothing up there save gray stone and a good view.

Their gaze was drawn to the south. Not far away was a mighty hill, almost a mountain.

"That is our next destination," the druid said.

"It's Brandwil's Seat?" Drom asked.

"It is, and there, I think, we will fulfill our quest or fail. At least the quest of the staff. But if we don't gain it, then our greater quest will fail also."

Drom studied the place. Its top was flat, and there were stone structures on it. The largest, by far, was a great ring of standing stones such as they had seen earlier on their travels. Close by was a single pillar by itself, tall, even and thin. Like a tree it seemed. At least one made of stone and without branches.

And then his thoughts slowed. He wondered if the others realized what he had. Like a stone tree it looked, but it might equally, or even more so, symbolize a staff.

He had no chance to say anything at that time though. Ariane spoke in a hushed voice beside them, her voice brimming with dread.

"Look below. It cannot be."

Drom glanced downward even as did the druid. There was a figure far below, outside the walls of the keep yet still in the great courtyard.

It raised a grim arm, and pointed straight at them like the finger of doom.

A chill went through Drom different from any he had ever felt.

"It is the druid Amrog."

"No," whispered Cadawn. "He is dead. We saw it. All three of us. Killed by the farmer."

178

Drom knew it was so, but the figure certainly looked like the druid. It must be another sent by the vizier though. Even so, the chill did not leave him.

24. Darkness in the Day

The long arm of the figure below withdrew, and whoever it was silently stepped into the shadows.

"I don't like this," Drom said. "Not even a little."

The sun was lowering, and the travelers had a choice to make. Stay in the fortress overnight, or risk going out into the wild. Neither alternative appealed.

They chose the fortress. They returned to the room below that had only one entry. It could be guarded, and guard it they did. The stairs were spread with rubble that would make noise should someone try to climb them, and they set a guard. All the while a spell of the druid glimmered over the floor, providing a soft light so that even should something pass unheard, it would not be unseen.

The night passed in mysterious silence. If it had been brooding in the land beyond, now it was oppressive like the feel of an approaching storm that promised tempests and destruction, but, as of yet, delivered not even a breeze.

It was a long night, and no one felt rested when the light of dawn relieved the eerie dark. There was no chorus of bird song, no chirping of insects, nor even much light. The sky was a sullen gray, deep with clouds yet giving no sign of approaching rain.

They watched the stairs and checked all the windows. There was no sign of the figure from last night outside. Strangely, that only unnerved them more.

Cold breakfasts were common for them, and they ate one more. Supplies were running low, and they divided small portions among themselves. There were no villages in this part of the land, and they must stretch out their food as much as possible, and gather what sustenance they could from the land while they traveled.

It was a strange feeling to leave the fortress. It had become dismal, yet in legend and story it was famous as a place of chivalry, might and a stronghold of the Light.

Of the figure, there was no sign, and outside they checked the flagstones where they had seen it. There were no tracks, but wind overnight had swept the stone of dust, so maybe they had been there but been dispersed.

They spoke no more of the strange sighting, but Drom knew they all kept thinking of it. Quickly they left the fortress behind them, and marched toward Brandwil's Seat.

The way was downward first, away from the fortress. But swiftly they began to ascend again. Their destination was a hill, and already they climbed its lower sides. Yet the top was much steeper, and at the summit a kind of tor, steeper than all the rest.

Darkness found them struggling up the side of the hill, having reached its round shoulders. In the twilight above the tor stood out, sheer in places and dangerous to climb, yet an ancient road coiled about it as a snake, and the very tip its head with the standing stones as fangs.

"I do not much like the idea of camping in this place," Cadawn said. "It would be folly to risk such a trail in the dark though."

Just as they had spent an uneasy night in the fortress, which they could see hulking in the distance on its own hill, they spent a restless one in the wild.

Their watch was good, for fear was on them. Three times they saw vague movement in the shadows, and once Cadawn let blaze druid light so that the entire shoulder of the hill was illuminated, yet it revealed nothing.

"A phantom maybe," Drom said.

181

"Yet one that wishes to be seen in the shadows, and not in the light."

"It taunts us," Ariane said.

Drom was becoming a little less anxious. If it were powerful, it would have struck. If it were an enemy, it likewise would have attacked. Most especially in the dark. It had done neither, so there was less reason to fear it when daylight swept the land.

By daylight though they saw something else. Around their camp, at a distance of a hundred paces, little cairns of stone had been set that were not there last evening.

"Is it a creature of faery?" Drom asked. His fear was returning, for it seemed now that whatever this thing was it truly just played with them.

Cadawn shook his head. "I think not. It is a man. Certainly it is a druid. For a ring of such stones is a terrible sign in our lore."

"They are used to mark druid cemeteries, are they not," Ariane said.

The druid did not answer. Instead, he straightened. "Come! We delay to no purpose. Our quest still lies before us, whatever our nighttime visitor intends. We are three and it is one. Every moment we tarry brings night closer, and by then I would be gone from this place. Another night such as the last might be one too many."

Now, more than ever, Drom missed the horses. Speed was better than a fight. Yet ever there was that part of him that wanted to test himself. Could he slay a phantom, if phantom it was, by courage and skill of steel?

They walked in silence up the winding track. Green grass grew to the sides, short but lush. The road was of chalky stone, made in antiquity yet looking today even as it must have in Brandwil's time.

The path was steep, and the walking was hard. The silence of the fortress was in this place too, and there was a feel of awe to it.

Drom was not religious, or at least not very. Even so, there was a sensation of presence here. There was no other way to describe it. He had seen many shrines to different gods. He had walked in churches. Even in the great cathedrals of cities he had stood, but this had a power beyond them all. He was silent, feeling a weight of holiness that he had never experienced before.

Into the quiet Ariane sang a hymn, and there was joy in her voice, and reverence as well as strength. Something inside her responded to the tor, but when she ceased the silence about them seemed even deeper.

There was fear, for whoever or whatever followed them must be nearby. Yet there was expectation also. The fortress had the weight of history and legend to it, and Drom respected those things. Yet they were powers of humanity. What he felt now was deeper than that. Older. Stronger. Beyond human comprehension, maybe, but not reverence.

The staff *must* be here. What else could give off such power?

They came to the top of the tor. It was not like a mountain peak, but rather it was fairly broad and mostly flat.

In the center was the ring of standing stones they had seen from afar. It was massive, and in good repair save for one stone that had developed a slight lean. Close by was a single pillar, taller and thinner than the rest. And on a shelf, just a little higher, was a strange formation of stone. It too was large, and it seemed natural, yet it also had the look of a bench. A bench such as a giant might use.

Cadawn spoke quietly, unwilling to disturb the peace of this place.

"To Brandwil's Seat first, I think. Of old, he used it as a lookout. Let us hope our eyes are open to see what may be seen."

The turf was very short and very green. They crossed it to what was called a seat, though it was some four feet wide and ten feet long. It was almost perfectly shaped, and Drom could not decide if it were made by hands or formed by nature.

The druid leaped up it, and Drom assisted Ariane. When she was standing upon the rock, he climbed up more slowly than the druid. All the walking was bringing out the pain in his left knee.

It was noon, and the sun was bright in a now cloudless sky. Even so, it seemed strangely darker than it should be.

Their view was excellent. The fortress seemed so close they could almost reach out and touch it. All around them too their view was just as good, and they beheld the realm of Camlanta as far as the eye could see.

Nothing moved, and it grew darker still.

"Away to the east," the druid said, "we can see foreign lands. All else is the soil of our people."

It was a fair view, and Drom felt love for his homeland stir. It was not perfect. Certainly its people were not. But for every type like the vizier or the king there were thousands of good, ordinary folk going about their business as best they could and intending harm to no one. It was the only land he knew, and the one he loved. Suddenly he knew he would fight for it. Not just to protect Ariane, but for its own sake.

Nothing gave any indication of the staff though. He was about to say as much, and turned to the druid.

Cadawn, however, was no longer looking around them but, shading his eyes, looking upward.

The darkness around them was growing, and it seemed unnatural.

"It should not be," Cadawn said. "It is an eclipse of the sun, yet according to the druid calculations there should not be one for another year."

Whatever the druid said, the sun was being edged out by the moon. Drom had experienced eclipses before, and read much more in the vizier's palace, but this was darker than what he had expected. It was eerie, and far away on the slopes of the hill some strange bird cried out. It was the only sound in all the wild, and it was not comforting.

It grew darker still, and at the peak of it, by instinct, druidic lore or foreknowledge, Cadawn lifted his arms and crossed them above his head.

Even as he did so it grew less dark, and a beam of light, faint but gold, pierced the skies and struck the hathlinden on his forearms.

The talismans blazed with light, turning the gold silver. A bell-like sound came from the metal, and as a shaft leaps from the bow a single ray, dazzlingly bright, shot through the air and struck at the base of one of the standing stones in the ring. It was the one that had developed a lean, and it cast the longest shadow.

Even as the light blazed, a change came over Ariane. She spoke, and yet it was not quite her voice.

"Hearken, ye defenders of the Light. The signs of doom gather, and while the darkness falls know also that in gloom is also the hour when light glimmers the brightest. All things are in a state of flux. Good and evil wax, and the troubled hearts of men can be swayed one way or the other. Follow the Light!"

Even as she spoke she pointed at the leaning standing stone. A moment all was bright, and then the light began to fade.

It was growing dark again, but the sun was returning. Drom had drawn his sword, for he sensed great magic. The voice was not Ariane's, but he could not decide who

185

it was. A god speaking through her? Aroth, maybe? Or perhaps the spirit of the druid Conhain, who had set this quest for them long ago.

The light faded. Drom felt the hilt of his sword thrum, and there was a warmth in the wood. Slowly, Cadawn lowered his arms and the light returned to normal, if an eclipse could be called such.

Yet there was movement behind the standing stones. The phantom figure they had seen at the fortress was visible, stalking up the ancient road.

"Who *is* it?" Ariane asked, her voice her own again.

"A demon from the otherworld," Drom answered.

"Nay," said Cadawn. "It is a druid sent by the vizier."

"And yet it looks like Amrog, the one we saw slain."

Ariane jumped down from the bench. "Perhaps it is all those things."

Drom jumped lightly down to join her. His aching knee was forgotten. A fight was looming, and the thrill of it ran through him.

Cadawn stepped down as well, and his face was troubled. The phantom figure stopped, and looked at them. Then his long arm pointed just as he had done at the fortress.

The figure spoke no words, but a sense of malice smote the travelers. To Drom, it felt like the gortha, yet different too. Whatever it was, it was more than druid. Yet even as he looked the figure, clad in tattered robes, pulled back its hood.

All was silence, and the sunlight kept growing. Several heartbeats passed, and then Cadawn hissed.

"It is Amrog. It can be no other. Dead, or somehow alive, it is him."

Ariane shook her head. "I think not. Dead, certainly. Possessing the body of Amrog, yes. But the druid himself? No. It is something else that wears his corpse as a skin."

For the first time, the figure made a noise. It was laughter, cold and terrible.

25. The House of the Flesh

Cadawn moved a little forward, and the strange figure did likewise.

"I don't understand, my brother druid," Cadawn said. "You are Amrog, yet I saw you die, or appear to. Yet you are here, and I beseech you to think of this. Was not Conhain the greatest druid of all? He dealt with the druids of Car Sagoth and the Court Druids equally and fairly, withholding counsel from neither. Can we follow his example and talk? We do not need to fight."

A moment the figure gazed at them, and then it answered.

"Speak not to Amrog. He is not here. I now dwell in the house of his flesh."

Ariane hissed. "It is a drachloss!"

Drom knew the word. Like so much else lately it was out of legend. In the stories a drachloss was a demon, and it possessed humans. Looking at this thing before him he could well believe it. Amrog was indeed dead.

"She that is born of my enemy understands, and I see the fear in her eyes. You will leave here, or die. I care not which. I am constrained to retrieve the staff you seek, and you have found it for me."

Cadawn took another step closer. "Who constrains you? What magic can command such as you?"

"He whom you call archdruid, or vizier. His spell-strength is great, aided by a goddess. Yet still I would seek the staff regardless. Aroth must not live again, and of the gods only Arofel understands my kind, and gives us leave

188

to do as we wish. Begone, for you have already lost this fight. You cannot kill that which is already dead."

"If I must, I will test that," Cadawn said.

Drom did not speak, but slowly drew deep breaths for what must come. He knew fighting was inevitable, but he feared this opponent.

Of them all, it was Ariane who attacked first. She stood still, but raised her right hand and from the palm a white light shone. Drom had seen this magic before, but it seemed stronger now. It was silver as the moon, and so bright that it should have pained his eyes to look upon. Yet it did not. Instead, he felt a sense of great peace, and nobility and something else beyond the reach of his thought.

The drachloss burned. Smoke rose in wisps from the flesh beneath the tattered robes. Blisters grew and peeled over his face. The skin reddened, and the tips of its fingers blackened.

It was disturbing to watch, yet the drachloss merely grinned at her.

"Holy light will not avail you. I care nothing for this house. When the abode no longer serves me, I shall reside within another. Until then, let it burn!"

As the creature spoke it raised its blackened fingers. What magic it had Drom did not know, and he was not going to wait to discover. If burning did not stop it, steel might. He leaped forward, blade in hand.

Drom's strike was not quick enough. The drachloss moved with greater speed than the druid Amrog could have done. It avoided him deftly but did not attack. Instead it raised a finger, and Ariane stumbled back, the silver light fading.

Drom felt a swell of wrath such as he seldom had before. Forward he strode, blade slashing, hacking and stabbing in a series of blows that few in the arena had ever withstood even momentarily.

The drachloss turned and twisted, evading, and then struck with a deadly-fast stab of his hand. It was not a punch. Rather it just touched Drom's shoulder, but immediately he felt the strength of his arm desert him.

"When I am finished with this body, perhaps I will use yours," the drachloss said. "Despite its age, it is still serviceable."

Cadawn yelled then. He voiced some ancient battle cry of the druids, and sent a stream of flame at the drachloss. Yet it was not only flame but also shadow. Like living ropes they each twined and curled together, fire and shadow, gripping, twisting, grasping.

Meshed in magic the drachloss burned. Drom, flipping the sword to his left hand, attacked again. The drachloss merely laughed though as fat melted from its body and a reek of dark smoke drifted upward. The stench of it was in Drom's nostrils as he struck.

The sword went deep. He withdrew it, and made to strike again, but the drachloss flung its arms out, sending flame and shadow scattering.

Standing there, smoke rising from its body, the drachloss laughed again. Once more Drom struck, but the creature used the bone of its arm to deflect the blow and then backhanded him across the face, sending him sprawling.

Drom came to his feet, fear rising in him as he stood. He knew now with certainty the creature only played with them. All three of them had attacked it, yet still it stood before them uncaring and unheeding of the wounds to the body it wore like a garment.

Even as he wondered what to do next he glanced at Ariane. Great strain showed on her face, and with both hands she pointed at the drachloss.

A wind sprang up, moaning within the ancient ring, and the standing stones themselves seemed to lean forward, caught by her power.

"Come hither, O druid of the court of the king. Return to mortal worlds, Amrog. I summon thee. And thou must answer. For I have the power."

The wind died. The standing stones cast grasping shadows, and the very tor on which they all stood trembled as though something moved, or parted, in the earth far below.

A chill cut the air, and there was a groan. From the mouth of the drachloss, or the earth itself, Drom was not sure. Supernatural dread hung in the air, and he knew that feeling and remembered that Ariane had cast this spell before. It was how she had raised the spirit of the enemy captain from death long ago near his farm.

He knew then what she was doing, and perceived the groan was from the drachloss. Now was the moment to act, and it would not last long.

Darting forward, he stabbed with the point of his sword. It took the enemy in the abdomen and drove upward, toward the heart. At the same moment Cadawn strode forward, and his hands went around the neck of the creature, twisting until bones popped.

The drachloss grinned, its face hideous. Then it laughed once more, but the sound was cut off and a voice replaced it. The voice of the druid Amrog.

"Mercy!"

"Now Drom!" Ariane shouted.

He knew what to do. The lore said two spirits could not inhabit the same body. Cadawn stepped back. And with a mighty stroke Drom beheaded the druid. It was the first step in ensuring the drachloss could not return to it, for the summoning of the spirit of Amrog had cast the drachloss out, if only momentarily.

191

The head rolled to the side, but the body stayed upright. Druid-fire blazed forth, and the corpse smoked and burned, hands grasping at the air.

After some moments, it fell. Yet the druid burned it until only bones remained. Even so, the drachloss was not defeated.

Drom felt a darkness gather upon him. His vision dimmed, and he fell to his knees. Even so, he still gripped his sword and the hilt was hot as with an inner fire.

He felt his body to be a vessel, and something tried to pour into it. If it did, his spirit would be displaced even as a glass of water that overflows. Against this he strove, and his body tensed and shook as he battled within his mind.

His mind was strong though. The vizier had discovered that. Ariane had learned it, and now the drachloss encountered it also. It found no entry.

Ariane placed her hands upon his shoulders. "This body is inviolate against you, drachloss. By the power of Aroth and the strength of the Light, I cast thee out. I cast thee from this land. I cast thee from this world!"

Drom felt the drachloss try to wrench free of him to find another host. He held it tight. Ariane continued to chant, and without a body to occupy its strength was diminished. It could not resist her power.

"I cast thee from life itself!" Ariane finished.

The drachloss faded, and a smoke, dark and shadowy, rose from around Drom's body and was dispelled into nothingness by the breeze.

"It is gone," Ariane said. "It will trouble no one for many long ages."

She let Drom go, and he stood. Ariane seemed weary, yet the druid was now intent on the standing stone.

"Quickly,' he said. "I doubt that the drachloss was the only plan of the vizier. We must retrieve the staff and go, for surely he knows where we are."

They had no tools with which to dig, but there were rocks with edges easy to hand and the soil was soft beneath the leaning standing stone.

26. Like a Coffin

Despite their weariness, the travelers dug swiftly with their rocks. They soon saw a rune emerge, carved into the very stone but hidden by soil.

Cadawn stood. "This is good. That is the druid mark for the letter "C.""

Drom stood and stretched his legs. "What does it signify?"

"I guess it stands for Conhain. And it means we are searching in the right place."

Ariane stood also. "Our effort is not in vain then. But it seems to me we might be digging for hours and hours."

After a little thought, Conhain answered. "I think you're right. Digging isn't the way, and judging by the lean of the stone I think it's been moved before. That which we seek may be deep underneath it. Anything else and Conhain would have risked the staff being discovered by chance."

"How else can we get to it except by digging?" Drom asked.

"The stone must be toppled. Only that way will we find what is underneath. Stand back."

Drom and Ariane did as asked. The druid stood motionless for a while, and then he summoned his magic. He lifted his arms, and the hathlinden gleamed.

Cadawn made no move. Yet Drom felt the earth beneath his feet thrum. Closer to the standing stone it split, and cracks ran deep into the earth. Almost gently the druid pushed his arms forward.

Slowly, gracefully, the standing stone began to move. A shiver went through it, and it seemed as though the earth itself rose and pushed it.

The stone toppled. The root of it had been sunk five feet deep, and the earth sprayed out as it came free. With a heavy thud it hit the ground, and the travelers carefully looked into the pit.

A box was set there, long like a coffin. Drom began to have doubts, but the druid was excited.

"See! The lid of the box has the same rune upon it."

Drom saw it then. Faint and obscured by dirt, yet it was there. They scrambled into the pit and lifted out the box. Going into the center of the ring they studied it. The timber was oak, but Cadawn told them it had been coated with preserving resin such as the druids knew how to prepare. And an enhancement of lasting was also upon it.

"It is for you to open, Archdruid Cadawn," Ariane said.

There were latches of brass, and he undid them with difficulty. Time and the elements had stiffened them. Then he opened the lid on its hinges, which also had become stiff.

Inside was a bear skin. "The druids regard bears as the king of animals," Cadawn muttered.

The skin was wrapped around an object by leather thongs. The druid undid them, and the bear fell dropped away.

In his hands was a staff. Six feet tall and perfectly cylindrical. It was the branch of a tree, yet the bark was gone. The bare timber was revealed, and it was white as snow and gleamed with light like the moon.

They felt the power of it. Peace was upon them, and the top of the tor, bathed in sunlight, seemed suddenly like an earthly paradise. The weariness dropped away from them, and joy filled their hearts.

The staff glowed suddenly bright, as did the hilt of Drom's sword, and then the light faded away and the staff grayed like any normal piece of timber.

"Do not be alarmed," the druid said. "Its power abides, but it veils itself so as not to draw attention to itself. We will need that as we travel."

He turned to Drom. "And now we know more about your sword hilt. If you remember, I said Conhain made multiple talismans from the timber of the tree of Aroth. Your hilt is one such. Treasure it."

Ariane looked knowingly at him, and Drom realized she suspected as much.

"Now what?" Drom said. "You have the staff, but how do we resurrect a god?"

No one had an answer. Yet Ariane spoke, and once more it was a voice that was not hers.

"Seek ye all the ancient home of the druids. In Losslach Grove summon the Great Druid. He will unlock your last quest."

The voice subsided, and Ariane seemed shocked. "It was not *me* who spoke."

Drom knew that. He also knew the quest was impossible. The ancient home of the druids was controlled by the Court Druids. It was the seat of power of their greatest enemy. Vizier. Archdruid. And servant of the Goddess of Chaos.

Thus ends *Sorcery Forged*. The Dream of the Druid series continues in book three, *Fate Forged*, where Drom and his companions will dare great deeds against impossible odds. And the vizier sets plans in motion to destroy them utterly…

FATE FORGED

BOOK THREE OF THE DREAM OF THE DRUID SERIES

COMING SOON!

Amazon lists millions of titles. Don't miss out when I release a new one. Join my Facebook group – *Home of High Fantasy* to keep up to date. There we also discuss all things epic fantasy – books, music and movies. It's a treasure hoard of the things we love!

Let me in, O Smaug the Magnificent!

No thanks. I'd rather doze on my treasure.

If Facebook groups aren't your thing, follow me on Amazon. Just go to one of my book pages, click my name near the title and then follow.

Dedication

There's a growing movement in fantasy literature. Its name is noblebright, and it's the opposite of grimdark.

Noblebright celebrates the virtues of heroism. It's an old-fashioned thing, as old as the first story ever told around a smoky campfire beneath ancient stars. It's storytelling that highlights courage and loyalty and hope for the spirit of humanity. It recognizes the dark – the dark in us all, and the dark in the villains of its stories. It recognizes death, and treachery and betrayal. But it dwells on none of these things.

I dedicate this book, such as it is, to that which is noblebright. And I thank the authors before me who held the torch high so that I could see the path: J.R.R. Tolkien, C.S. Lewis, Terry Brooks, Susan Cooper, Roger Taylor and many others. I salute you.

And, for a time, I too shall hold the torch high.

Appendix: Encyclopedic Glossary

Camlanta is an ancient land, yet the gathering of tribes into a single kingdom, ruled by a sole chieftain-become-king, occurred not much sooner than it did with those tribes that migrated eastward and formed their realms close to the sea.

These two groups of peoples became sundered, yet shared a common origin neither forgot. The people in the old lands, in many ways, stayed truer to their ancestral culture. The tribes that migrated, and splintered in their turn into more kingdoms, came into greater contact with the elves. They changed, yet still they remembered the lore of their forefathers. The name of Camar, for these people wherever their dwelling, is used with pride by them all.

Camlanta was not untouched by elvish contact either. The Halathrin, for such do the elves name themselves, were once more widely traveled than they are now. Presently, they fortify their forest stronghold, and gather their strength for great trials to come. One day, perhaps soon, they will walk the land more openly again.

Perhaps it is the druids of Camlanta that best represent the culture as it persists in the kingdom. The Court Druids have forgotten much lore, but acquired new powers from service to Arofel. The loyal druids of Car Sagoth remain true to a long line of druidic knowledge that predates even the Shadowed Wars. Yet they acquired new lore too, and incorporated it into the culture rather than changing. They have had much contact with the shamans of the Cheng Empire and the lòhrens of the eastern realms.

These two forces of loyalty and change vie with each other throughout the realm. The people are proud of their heritage, yet also they envy the tribes that migrated and forged new realms in lands untrodden by other men. And the gods, like the people, are torn in mind. And they vie one against another…

List of abbreviations:

Cam. Camar

Comb. Combined

Cor. Corrupted form

Hal. Halathrin

Prn. Pronounced

Alithoras: *Hal.* "Silver land." The Halathrin name for the continent they settled after leaving their own homeland. Refers to the extensive river and lake systems they found and their wonder at the beauty of the land.

Amrog: *Cam.* "Divine fire." A mid to high ranking, but ambitious, Court Druid.

Ariane: *Cam.* "Beloved daughter." Current high priestess of the Cult of Aroth.

Arofel: *Cam.* "Star flash – a meteorite." Goddess of Chaos, and sister to Aroth.

Aroth: *Cam.* "The sun." God of creation and order. Of all the gods, the only to become incarnate and dwell among humanity in an attempt to better them. Slain by the machinations of Arofel.

Asarte: *Cam.* "Cold of the void." Goddess of warriors and tricksters. A favorite of gladiators.

Brandwil's Fortress: The chief fortress and capital of an ancient ruler of Camlanta. It was within it that the last battle of a terrible civil war played out. Yet the fortress, the period of time, and the figure of Brandwil are remembered in legend as being of a golden era. It is prophesied this ancient hero will return in the land's darkest hour.

Brandwil's Seat: A lookout close to Brandwil Fortress.

Broken Lands (the): An area of Camlanta ravished by battle and dark sorcery during the Shadowed Wars.

Cadawn: *Cam.* "Battle joy." Archdruid. Leader of the druids of Car Sagoth. Young to hold the position, yet the greatest druid in living memory.

Camalduin: *Cam.* "Camar woods." The capital city of Camlanta. Once a mighty forest, of which wild vestiges still remain in the hinterlands.

Camar: A race of interrelated tribes with a common culture. Some remained in their original homeland, of which Camalduin was the heart, and others migrated in stages and established cities along a broad stretch of eastern Alithoras.

Camlanta: *Cam.* "Land of the Camar." The ancient realm of the Camar people after separate tribes formed a single kingdom.

Car Sagoth: *Cam.* "Ghost mist – the land of mists and ghosts." A lowland area of swamp and mire that forms the guarded domain of the loyal druids. In antiquity, great battles were fought here. Some say the Shadowed Wars were but the last battles, and that many were contested before between peoples that none now remember, unless the druids retain secret knowledge they do not share.

Careth Tar: *Cor. Hal.* "Careth Tar(an) – Great Father." Title of respect for the leader of the lòhrens (wizards of the east).

Castanuin: *Cam.* "Glint of the sea." Archdruid of the Court Druids. Of royal blood, though distantly.

Catagern: *Cam.* Etymology contested. "Sharp peak." A farmer and one-time neighbor of Drom.

Cheng Empire: A land to the north of Camlanta. Ruled by shamans for a great period. In turn, they were overthrown by an empress. Now ruled by an elected government.

Conhain: *Comb. Cam* & *Hal.* First element unknown, though possibly "noble or royal." The second "hero." Accounted the greatest of druids in recorded history. However he was not just a druid but also descended from the first king of Camlanta via a daughter.

Conmah: *Cam.* "Noble horse – though this etymology is disputed". The current king of Camlanta.

Conmast: *Cam.* Etymology of "con" contested. "Noble harvest." Grandson of the first king of Camlanta.

Cult of Aroth: A group of believers - secretive, persecuted, heroic, who are led by the High Priestess of Aroth. They believe salvation lies with the god Aroth, and they work toward his arising from death.

Dagdor (The): One of the gods. Associated with farming, beer and magic. Said to be kindhearted, and to befriend travelers in need.

Drachloss: *Cam.* "Shadow spirit." A demon. Some hold demons to be of the world of faery. Others place them as akin to the gods.

Dragons: Creatures of faery. Curious. Powerful. Said to love riddles. They can breathe fire, ice or both.

Dragon-fire Peak: The greatest peak of the Tainglint Mountains. Famed in story and song, though few know where truth ends and legend begins.

Drom: An ex-gladiator of the arena. His fighting name was Isarn the Invincible. One of the few warriors to survive multiple bouts, and the only gladiator in modern times to go beyond seven, for surviving seven means the gladiator becomes a free man and can leave fighting behind him. At one time an associate of the king, vizier and nobility. Now a hunted outlaw, pursued by a vendetta that does not sleep.

Dromdruin: *Cam.* "Valley of the ancient woods." Full name of Drom.

Druid: A person of lore, wisdom and magic. Their order arose from the merchant class. In the days prior even to the Shadowed Wars merchants were the only people who frequently traveled the land. Thus they were often called upon to settle disputes, being unfamiliar with the parties involved and therefore independent. This gave them great power, which some merchants began to specialize in, and they traveled the land no longer as traders but as bringers of knowledge and justice.

East March (the): The east border of Camlanta. Largely depopulated in antiquity when many Camar tribes immigrated eastward to coastal regions far away.

Ebona: *Cam.* Once a goddess. She has long since left her birthing lands.

Elug: See goblins.

Elves: See Halathrin.

Elù-haraken: *Hal.* "The shadowed wars." Long ago battles in a time that is become myth.

Escaping fish (the): A fighting move from the arena that constitutes a zigzag motion.

Faery: The otherworld, and the creatures that live in it. They are beings of magic from the earliest days of the earth, and kin to gods. Some are malevolent while others are benevolent. Most are indifferent. They existed before humanity, but their power diminished. When humanity is spent, they will return and shape the land to what it was before. In the meantime, they hide in dark places, and have strongholds called sidhe. From these strongholds they rarely venture, unless summoned by great magic or their own designs require it.

Faestone: A talisman from the world of faery. They are rare, potent in magic and forbidden for mortals by the goddess Arofel. Some speculate this is because they are forces of power that corrupt, and even the goddess of chaos disapproves of them. Others suggest that the goddess is in conflict with the rulers of faery.

Falassa: The goddess of story and speech. Some claim she is the greatest in power of all the gods.

Gahranrir: *Cam.* "White elf." The wife of Brandwil. Legend claims her of faery or elven descent.

Goblin: Creatures of the Shadowed Wars. Steeped in evil. They favor mountain caves as their dwellings, and delve far and deep. Fierce warriors in a group, yet tending to cowardice by themselves.

Goddess of Chaos: See Arofel.

Gorik: *Cam.* "Boar strength." Captain of a band of dwarves. Dwarves keep their own language secret and adopt the language of the humans they deal with for public use.

Gortha: *Cam.* "The hungry one." A type of faery creature. Malevolent, powerful and wielder of the strongest weapon of all – fear. Associated with war and pestilence, but mostly famine.

Halath: *Hal.* King of the Halathrin. He died long ago. He led his people on their exodus to Alithoras, and was revered and loved as a great ruler.

Halathrin: *Hal.* "People of Halath." A race of elves named after an honored lord who led an exodus of his people to the land of Alithoras in pursuit of justice, having sworn to defeat a great evil. They are human, though of fairer form, greater skill and higher culture. They possess a unity of body, mind and spirit that enables insight and endurance beyond the native races of Alithoras. Said to be immortal, but killed in great numbers during their conflicts in ancient times with the evil they sought to destroy. Those conflicts are collectively known as the Shadowed Wars.

Halls of Lore: Essentially, a library within the stronghold of the lòhrens (wizards) in northern Alithoras. It serves as a repository for the known history of humanity and the wisdom of the ages.

Hathlinden: *Hal.* "Bands of the radiant moon." Talismans forged by the Halathrin in the deeps of time. Stolen by sorcerers, retrieved by wizards, gifted to the dwarves, hoarded by the dragon Rah-essen after his destruction of the dwarven settlement at Dragon-fire Peak. Retrieved by the druid Conhain.

Hobgoblin: A variety of goblin, taller and shrewder than most.

Hrakash: "Elves" in goblin tongues. It can be translated as blades of light and death.

Isarn the Invincible: The fighting name of Drom in the arena. Early in his career known just as Isarn, which signifies iron.

Kentanos: *Cam.* "From the border." A dwarf in Gorik's band.

Kingdom of Light: A promised life after death for those who strive toward betterment. At least according to

Aroth. The other gods say different things and have different names for eternal life.

Korrig: *Cam.* "Small but mighty." Another name for dwarves.

Lòhren: *Hal. Prn.* Ler-ren. "Knowledge giver – a counselor." Other terms used by various nations include sage, wizard, and druid.

Losslach Grove: *Cam.* "Restless leaves." A grove in the Halduin Forest. An ancient place where the magic of the earth is strong, and the borders between worlds is weak.

Magic: Mystic power.

Maramne: *Cam.* "Beloved." Mortal wife of Aroth, and the first high priestess, from whom all others are descended. Also known as The Teacher.

Merem: *Cam.* "Cherished." A descendant of Maramne, but not a high priestess. Mother of Ariane.

Morrigan: *Cam.* "Strife queen." A powerful being from the world of faery.

Naahat: *Cam.* "The road that ends." The god of death. Also sleep, tranquility and rest.

Norhanu: A foreign word, borrowed in antiquity along with philosophy and magic. "Serrated blade." A psychoactive herb.

Pendraig: *Cam.* "Head of the tribes or armies". An ancient term for a chief elected to lead multiple tribes during times of war.

Queen of Battles: See Morrigan.

Rah-essen: *Hal.* "Fire-ice." The dragon who formerly had his lair at the top of Dragon-fire Peak. All dragon names are prefixed with the word "rah."

Rathglen: *Cam.* "Ring of steel." A warrior of antiquity. He and Conhain slew the dragon Rah-essen.

Serpent coils: A martial maneuver, used in weapon and bare-hand fighting, that feigns retreat only in order to set up an attack.

Shadowed Lord: Once a lòhren. But he succumbed to evil and pursued forbidden knowledge and powers. He created an empire of darkness and struck to conquer all Alithoras during the elù-haraken. He was defeated, but his magic had become greater than any ever known. Some say he will return from death to finish the war he started. Whether that is so, no one knows. But the order of lòhrens guard against it, and many evils that served him yet live.

Shadowed Wars: See elù-haraken.

Sidhe: A mound of faery. Mound is a loose term. A sidhe can also be a hill, or a mountain. Sometimes, it's even a body of water. Essentially it refers to a stronghold of a creature, or community, of faery.

Tainglint Mountains: *Cam.* "Thrust of swords." A long mountain chain in the north of Camlanta. According to legend, populated by creatures of faery, including dragons and dwarves.

Tainlin: *Cam.* "Leaping light." A Court Druid.

Tassalind: *Cam.* "Light on the tossing sea." An assassin, currently in the employ of the king.

Tathgar: *Cam.* "Pine-scented air." A druid of Car Sagoth.

The Teacher: See Maramne.

Tree of Aroth: The tree against which the god Aroth was slain by spear thrusts.

Vaceran: A word in the secret speech of the arena. It signifies "I will win."

Vizer: A high official of government. Not a native Camar term. The position and word is borrowed from neighboring realms.

Warrior-spell (the): A spell of druidry that enhances hate, martial drive and courage. Those under the influence lose all sense of danger, and die swiftly either in battle or by hastened biological aging. Forbidden by the druids of Car Sagoth. Used at times by the Court Druids.

Wizard: See lòhren.

About the author

I'm a man born in the wrong era. My heart yearns for faraway places and even further afield times. Tolkien had me at the beginning of *The Hobbit* when he said, ". . . one morning long ago in the quiet of the world . . ."

Sometimes I imagine myself in a Viking mead-hall. The long winter night presses in, but the shimmering embers of a log in the hearth hold back both cold and dark. The chieftain calls for a story, and I take a sip from my drinking horn and stand up . . .

Or maybe the desert stars shine bright and clear, obscured occasionally by wisps of smoke from burning camel dung. A dry gust of wind marches sand grains across our lonely campsite, and the wayfarers about me stir restlessly. I sip cool water and begin to speak.

I'm a storyteller. A man to paint a picture by the slow music of words. I like to bring faraway places and times to life, to make hearts yearn for something they can never have, unless for a passing moment.

Printed in Dunstable, United Kingdom